HIS EROTIC EMASCULATION

Riley Rose

ISBN: 9798866209491

This is a work of fiction. Names, characters, businesses, places, events and incidents are either the products of the author's imagination or used in a fictitious manner. Any resemblance to actual persons, living or dead, or actual events is purely coincidental.

See all Riley Rose books on author page author.to/rileyrosewriter
Contact Riley Rose by email at rileyrosewriter@gmail.com

Warning: These are fictional stories written in a fantasy context. Don't try any of what you are about to read at home. This writing is of a mature nature and not intended for sensitive or underaged readers.

The Mechanic's Cuck

"Lewis, go make me a sandwich."

Mackenzie called out loudly from beneath the frame of a nineteen-sixty-seven Chevrolet Camaro sporting flame-decals which cut brightly across the black-glossy paint. Lewis looked longingly down at her body which lay sprawled out beneath the classic muscle car as she raised both her arms up under the vehicle into the transmission block to install a new clutch assembly. Tattoos of crowns, tribal symbols, dragons, skulls, and flames decorated both her arms creating a near full sleeve of artwork.

Her large breasts, barely covered in her white-tank top, flexed upwards propelled along by the muscular pull of her arms thus heightening her appeal. Beyond this impressive display of strength and womanhood, her long, curvaceous legs protruded from Daisy-duke short shorts. The thinnest bit of tattered denim spread as wide as it possibly could across the opening of her vagina giving only the tiniest veneer of privacy as her legs spread out wide along either side of the rolling cart on which she lay. Lewis's heart pounded and his cock throbbed at the thought of kneeling down and just sliding a deft little finger in around the edge of that slender shorts hem to touch the delicate and wet tissues underneath. In his dreams, he pondered pressing a furtive tongue against such delicious womanhood and maybe even rendering some pleasure to her.

She rolled the cart down from the underside of the car and snarled, "what are you staring at?"

"You're beautiful." He murmured, weakly.

She squinted at him and replied, "and you're pathetic. Now get to it. My lunch-break is coming up and I didn't marry you just to have you lurking around my shop."

Lewis turned to leave the shop as the bell over the old wooden door dinged letting him know that a customer was arriving. He kept walking, not wishing to witness another one of Mackenzie's interactions with her seemingly never-ending stream of customers. Lewis probably wouldn't have minded it so much except she never even bothered to treat him the way she treated the jock-boy gearheads that would frequent the shop. They hardly ever seemed to actually buy anything or order any repairs. They all just came…

…for her.

Mackenzie licked her lips at the sound of the bell and hastily slapped the clutch-plate into place making a mental note to return to secure it later. Like a dog salivating for Pavlov's treatment, Mackenzie's vagina already grew wet at the thought of which hunk it would get to taste the flavor of today. Mackenzie slid out and hastily wiped her hands with an old cotton rag slightly smudging off a bit of the black grease that covered them. It didn't matter. Mackenzie knew that other girls needed clean hands, pretty hair, makeup, and shit like that because they were weak and pathetic. All they did was sit around at home waiting for the phone to ring like a bunch of lonely losers. It was just as well they preened and waited because that meant even more boys for Mackenzie. Once she got a hold of one of those throbbing cocks pulsing out the best that a man had to offer, it was only a matter of time before she could milk the owner dry and make him collapse forsaking all other women save for her. Sex for them would never be the same again because it wouldn't be sex with Mackenzie, and she knew it too. She had lost track of how many cocks she had consumed by mouth or by pussy, but she knew that whatever dick-possessor had just ran her bell was as slated to become her next victim as a lamb being lead to the slaughter.

She stood up and saw an older teenage boy leering at her creepily.

Mackenzie blinked in surprise at first and then a wry smile came to her face. One thing she loved about teenagers was every year she kept getting older, but every year they stayed the same age. It was nice, however. She liked it when naïve boys brought her fresh virgin cocks to destroy.

"What's your name, kid?" She asked.

"Is it true what they say about you?" He asked back. She twisted her voluptuous lips up thoughtfully and sized up this kid. He wore tight jeans, a white-t-shirt and a mischievous smile. Greasy black hair topped him off and he had a bit of cocky swagger to his stance. Despite this, his hand trembled nervously, and Mackenzie could smell the aromatic stench of virginity on him. Mackenzie reached down and snapped her shorts button letting them fall down her legs revealing her fully shaved pussy. The kid's eyes widened in shock as she stepped casually out of her shorts and put a hand against his chest pushing him back. He had not expected this.

"Yeah. What your buddies giggled about in the back of the locker room during your circle-jerk is true about me. So, now that you're here, what you going to do about it, stud?" She kept pushing him backwards this whole time making him retreat awkwardly through her shop as she gently pushed him back to her waiting room with its conveniently oversized couches.

"I…uh…uh… my name is Jeremy." He stammered out awkwardly.

"Everyone calls me Mac. So, Jeremy, have you ever sucked a girl's clit before?"

"No… uh… no ma'am."

"I told you my name's Mac, not Ma'am! Get on your knees."

Jeremy fell to his knees next to a small coffee table in the waiting room which boasted about a dozen Motor Week magazines. Mackenzie grabbed the back of his head as she thrust her hips forward. "Then it's time for you to stick your tongue out and taste a real woman for a change." Jeremy did as he was instructed, and Mac smiled lightly as his soft pink tongue caressed her clit delicately.

"Ohh… good boy. You're a natural." She murmured as she continued to grind her crotch on his face. "That's it. Keep licking to get may vag' good and ready to eat your cock. Give a nice wet kiss to the vagina that's going to take your virginity away so hard that no other girl will ever be able to please you again."

Jeremy softly placed his hands on the inked flesh of either side of Mackenzie's hips. For a moment, Mackenzie feared he might push her back in a vain attempt to free his face from her pussy, but instead he curled his fingers around the flesh of her buttocks and pulled her in reaching his tongue even further back and curling the tip of it lightly inside of her.

"Ooh… eager boy." Mackenzie groaned in pleasure. She looked down and playfully ran her fingers through his hair saying "I'm wet enough now. Break out that tool in your pants and show me what kind of caliber it is." Jeremy shivered with anticipation as beads of sweat ran down his forehead. He rose to his feet, eagerly unclasped his large belt-buckle, and shoved his pants down letting his ten-inch cock swing out.

"Nice!" Mackenzie hissed out through gritted teeth as she beheld the purple-tipped veiny shaft. She swung her hand underneath and grabbed his nuts giving them a soft squeeze which brought a look of fear and shock to his face as he started to press away from her. She shushed him saying "just checking under your hood. Don't be afraid. I ain't gonna hurt you. If I broke your manhood now, what would I have to play with later."

She casually slid him onto one of her couches where he laid out with his massive erection sticking straight up at the ceiling. A mixture of hope and panic stood out in his expression and for a moment

Mackenzie just stared down at him with a smile. She loved this moment, the moment before she takes a new boy and teaches his cock what it feels like to be a man. She loved that look of pathetic virtue on their faces as they realize what is soon to come and they both simultaneously dread it and secretly hope for it. It's the last time in their lives they will make such an expression as her pussy would soon swallow their dick whole making them wince in fear at the implications of what had just happened. Then she would cover their mouths, as she doesn't like being distracted during a good fucking. She would watch their eyes as they make that beautiful transition from fear to resistance to acceptance as they lose all will and succumb to their innate desire to submissively let her have her way with their soft and warm bodies. It didn't matter what the man was like, they all fell to her the same way. Soon, each and every one would keep coming back to Mac's Garage as Mackenzie would keep them cumming again and again.

"Get in me, loser. We're fucking." Mackenzie said with a cocky sneer as she straddled Jeremy. She centered her hips and took a sweet little seat right on top of his delicious cock. He started to say something, but she shoved her left hand over his mouth and pinned his arm down with her right hand. She stared into his eyes with a sinister smile as she began pumping away at his massive manhood with her hips. Mackenzie couldn't lie, even to herself, about how impressed she felt with Jeremy's cock. The monster banged around the inside of her vagina stretching out every single wall in a tasty manner making her feel nicely filled. She ground against this, feeling his cock pulsating away deep inside her as she pressed her sensitive clitoris, well primed by his tongue, against the tiny patch of treasure-trail just north of his cock feeling the warm flesh and soft-bristled hairs tickle her womanhood. For his part, Jeremy actually started to fight back against this, seemingly having encountered a change of mind as he started to feebly push against her.

"Shh… just let it go. You stepped into my garage and now your virginity is mine to take." Mackenzie whispered to him.

His eyes flashed with fear and confusion.

"Once you squirt it in me, it will be over. You'll have lost your virginity on an old couch in the back of a car-shop. It doesn't matter if you do it now or after a few hundred more pumps. I'm going to keep fucking you until you can't hold back anymore. You're going to feed my womanhood with that firehose you got between your legs. It's just a matter of time, now. But go ahead, I kind of prefer if you try resisting for a while. That makes this more fun for me."

She continued to pump and grind against him until he succumbed to her desire and began pumping in tempo along with her. She loved that moment, when a man gives up and decides the only course of action left for him is to enjoy the experience while it lasts. Sadly, it didn't last long as after a few more pumps he stiffened incredibly hard inside her, and she felt him grunt against her hand as he filled her core full of semen. She slowed down her thrusts, letting him finish cumming inside her, as he collapsed back exhausted and exhilarated.

"Well, that's disappointing. All cock and no endurance. Spend some time practicing on stretching out those scrawny little high school sluts until you learn how to fuck proper, then come back to me when you're ready."

She pulled herself up feeling him wetly slide right out of her. She stepped lightly over to where her shorts lay on the ground and bent over the grab them. As she did this, she turned around to see him admiring her full, womanly ass and gave him a wink saying, "when you're ready to return, don't forget, my legs are always open here at Mac's garage."

"Can't forget that clutchplate." Mac whispered to herself as she slid her shorts back on while walking the short hallway which lead from where she worked to where she lived. She arrived in the kitchen, a quaint little chrome and avocado green job reminiscent of a bygone era of atomic bombs and atomic blondes. Here, Lewis sat morosely at the table next to a ham and pickle sandwich.

"I don't like it." Lewis said to her out of nowhere.

"What?" Mackenzie asked.

Lewis grimaced and his face blushed beet red with a mix of jealousy and anger as he continued, "I don't like you sleeping with other men."

Mackenzie looked at him closely for a second letting the pregnant pause of silence fill the air. She answered, "I'm naturally going to fuck other men. It's not like you can please me." She went over to the sink and began washing her hands properly.

"You don't even give me the chance to." Lewis complained.

"Are you begging for a chance for your four-inch pecker."

Lewis looked down sadly.

Mackenzie shrugged saying, "like I said. It's not like you can please me."

Later that night…

Moonlight glinted down through the open window. Outside, bugs chirped their never-ending mating songs of horniness while distant cars filled with disenchanted teenagers roared into the night along the tracks of their impromptu street races. Mackenzie's naked body lay sprawled across the queen-sized bed.

Lewis in his striped pajamas stared at her from the shadows.

She appeared almost as a pantomime of an Egyptian hieroglyph, with one arm raised and bent at the elbow while the other was bent back in the other direction in her casual sprawl across what was supposed to be their matrimonial bed. Lewis allowed his eyes to trail along the bulging ripples of her surprisingly well-defined muscles and onto the womanly curves of her breasts as they slowly raised and lowered with each of her slumbering breaths. The square-cut moonlight cast across her pale body made the black ink of her tattoos, scrawled reminders of adventures and events the likes of which she had never bothered to explain to Lewis, stand out in fresh contrast with the somber illumination.

Lewis watched his wife from the shadows.

She was his wife, damn it.

He should be able to have sex with her.

With ninja-like stealth, Lewis slid off his pajama pants letting them softly fall to the ground with the subtlest of *whiff* sounds. Soon after, his underwear and buttoned pajama shirt followed along the same path to the ground leaving him naked just like his wife. His soft, petite body glowed lightly in the moonlight. Once upon a time, in some vain effort to impress Mackenzie, he had ventured to shave away all body hair leaving him smooth as a newborn.

"That's what married people do, right? They get naked in bed together." Lewis whispered to himself to bring courage to his mind. Mackenzie looked like a sleeping panther to his eyes, but his throbbing erection left him no choice but to risk it and try to have sex with his wife.

Lewis's heart throbbed in his chest with panicked fear as his cock trembled with anticipation. He cautiously approached the bed like a rabbit walking towards a wolf's den. Mackenzie groaned lightly and rolled to her side a bit causing Lewis to freeze in terror. Soon, however, soft flutters of snoring came to her breath giving Lewis fresh reassurance. Lewis slowly approached again and came level to her with the bed. He gently began to slide his right knee onto the bed moving slowly to keep from creaking the wood frame or causing too noticeable of a dip in the mattress. Inch-by-inch he shifted his weight onto his right knee. He carefully watched Mackenzie's chest rise and fall and he slowly timed his movements to match her breathing. Her perky nipples, supple flesh, widely spaced hips, with her ever-hungry vagina between them, gave him thrilling sensations of desire which drove him to take such risks.

Lewis began to bring his left knee up onto the bed so that he would be on top of it, alongside his wife. Quick as a flash, Mackenzie's hand dropped from where it lay and swung in between his legs. Before he could react, she snapped her hand upwards between his legs and quickly found his testicles with her fingers. She squeezed them hard bringing a whimper of pain to his mouth as he collapsed forward catching himself with his hands. His face contorted as he stared intimately into the eyes of his wife as she held his manhood in her painful, vice-like grip.

"Lewis? What are you doing here?" Mackenzie demanded as she maintained a firm and painful hold of his testicles.

"Noth… nothi…" Lewis began to stutter and whimper.

She gave and extra hard squeeze which caused him to cry out in pain.

"Don't lie to me like I'm stupid. That's not the kind of relationship we have, Lewis." Mackenzie said firmly. Tears formed at the corners of his eyes as Lewis shivered on the edge of crying.

She relaxed her grip as he sniffed back sobs and she continued in a more measured voice all the while still holding onto his testicles, "why did you come to my bed? Tell the truth."

"I wanted to have sex with you." Lewis confessed.

Mackenzie stared at him silently for a moment. She neither squeezed harder nor released her grasp of his testicles keeping them ever so slightly in pain.

She sighed sadly and said, "this is a problem I'm going to have to fix. Isn't it?"

"Why can't I have sex with you?"

Mackenzie pursed her lips and replied, "Once a boy fucks a girl, he leaves. That's why they're fun for a moment or two, but not any longer."

"But we're married. You're my wife." Lewis protested.

Mackenzie replied, "Don't worry, Lewis. I know how to fix this problem. I know how to fix you. Do you trust me?"

Lewis sniffed back a tear. Mackenzie reached down with her other hand and ran it alongside his rock-hard erection saying, "you like being squeezed like this, don't you?"

Lewis shuddered and held his silence unable to respond.

"It's okay. You don't have to be afraid to say it." Mackenzie prompted.

"It hurts." Lewis said.

"No, Lewis, they hurt. These things are hurting you. And I'm going to fix that tonight. Wait here. I'll be right back to take care of you."

With that said, Mackenzie let go of Lewis's nuts bringing a gasp of relief to his mouth. She sat up and slid out of bed letting him collapse down in her place. Lewis felt the residual warmth of her hot body and smelling the scent of her essence on the sheets.

"Shh… I'll get you taken care of. Just wait a few minutes while I get some supplies."

"Supplies?" Lewis asked.

"You'll see what I mean soon enough."

Mackenzie disappeared into the darkness of the hallway for what felt like an eternity. Dutifully, Lewis lay there in the moonlight on her bed painfully alone in a place he had worshipfully desired. He reached down and felt his testicles with his hand and pondered her question. Had he liked her squeezing his testicles? The residual pain still throbbed through his manhood and yet somehow it felt fulfilling and cleansing all at once. Almost as if he could bring her sexual pleasure by experiencing pain, and that would be satisfying enough for him. Lewis pondered this new development, and it brought a strange sense of relief to his mind. His pitiful existence would be justified by the pain he would experience on behalf of his goddess. Some strange duality of the nature of pain and sex began to form within his mind. They were both merely sensations created by touch, and yet one was considered desirable while the other terrible. Lewis wondered if he did enjoy pain, so he gave a little test squeeze of his own testicles. They just throbbed dully and then he could squeeze them no further. It seemed as if his own hand wouldn't obey him in some bodily sense of self-preservation. More importantly, it just hurt. He didn't experience any of the strange sense of submissive fulfillment from it when he did it himself.

"You're still here." Mackenzie said from the doorway.

Lewis rolled over feeling self-conscious about how his firmly erect cock bounced and swayed as he moved in a somewhat embarrassing manner. Lewis gritted his teeth and held his silence. Mackenzie looked powerful, almost panther-like as she stood naked in the doorway half clad in bright moonlight half concealed in darkness. She stepped forward and her breasts swayed lightly as she moved while her hips shifted back and forth seductively bringing her body more fully into the moonlight. Lewis let his eyes trail down along the fine curves of her delicious frame to the beautiful little lips of her crotch and dreamed about the sensation of her swallowing his manhood with those wetly sensual lips. He pictured it in her mind but all he could conjure was her harumphing in arrogant annoyance and laughing at him after he cum after only a few pumps and barely managed to fill her pussy at all with his manhood. His erection started to decrease as he considered this. He let his eyes shift over to her muscular arms, rendered powerful from long days of machine-work and automobile repair.

She was going to use those arms to hurt him.

His cock stiffened at the thought, as she continued "you didn't run away. That means you did like it, didn't you?"

He licked his lips and replied, "I… I'm not sure."

She nodded and said, "This is something I've been wanting to do to you for a long time, but never really worked up the nerve to do until tonight." She gently sat down on the side of the bed and held up a small metal ring featuring a series of angular perforations along with a tightening screw.

"A car part?" Lewis asked in confusion.

"For you." Mackenzie replied firmly.

Lewis lowered an eyebrow "Huh?"

"I want you to wear this hose clamp for me."

"I don't understand." Lewis said.

"Once I put it on you, it will make sense."

"Okay." Lewis replied hesitantly.

Mackenzie slowly got into bed with him sitting on her knees between his legs with his manhood sprawled open and vulnerable in front of her. She reached down and her thin fingers cupped Lewis's testicles bringing forth a fresh gasp of anticipation and fear to his lips.

"Shhh… relax, I'm not going to hurt you with my fingers anymore tonight." Mackenzie whispered.

She slid the metal circular clamp around both of Lewis's testicles slightly across the top of them so they couldn't slip out. She then produced a stubby screwdriver and started tightening the screw on the clamp gripping it ever more tightly around Lewis's nuts.

Lewis whimpered and flexed trying to get away.

"This is something you need, Lewis. Trust me." Mackenzie said to him with a sense of firm intimacy in her voice.

"I lied at our wedding. I wasn't ready to love you. At least, not the way you were then. I can't ever love a boy. They come, then they cum, then they leave. Best to not get to attached. Do you understand?" Mackenzie said.

"Then why did you marry me?" Lewis asked.

"Because I saw promise in you to be something else. Something more." Mackenzie said gently.

"After tonight, I will be able to love you. But my love comes with a price. A price that up until now I wasn't sure you would be able to pay. A price I wasn't sure I wanted to make you pay. But knowing a part of you enjoys the pain changes everything." Mackenzie said as she steadied the screwdriver once again and asked, "are you able to pay the price of my love?"

Lewis drew a deep breath to steady himself as he nodded.

Mackenzie tightened the screw drawing the ring closed hard around Lewis's testicles. He cried out and grabbed a hand over his mouth to cover his scream. His body felt as if it would explode from the hideous pain and yet his mind felt as if it would explode from the joy at being able to provide Mackenzie with such pleasure. For her part, she panted lightly even though turning the screw had hardly cost her any exertion at all as she smiled broadly saying, "oh my god, that feels incredible. I've never felt so close to anyone in my life. You doing okay so far?"

Lewis gritted his teeth and nodded.

"I want to just keep twisting this screw until they burst off you, but let's not rush this. One more turn for tonight, then you wear the clamp for me the rest of tomorrow. Understand?"

Lewis nodded.

Mackenzie turned the screw one more time. This time Lewis shouted in pain as his knees buckled upward from the agonizing sensation of the sharp-edged metal crushing his testicles together. Mackenzie tossed the screwdriver aside onto the floor and pushed down on Lewis's knees to flatten them back out as she said, "Shh… shh… you did it. You did it. That's enough for tonight."

Tears of agony and joy streamed down Lewis's face.

Mackenzie purred in ecstasy as she said, "I never thought in a million years I would get the chance to do this."

She gently lifted his swollen testicles and inspected them in the moonlight saying "they're so badly damaged. Can you even feel them anymore?"

Lewis nodded.

"Hmmm… I'm sure that will go away soon enough." Mackenzie said. She slid her body forward and brought Lewis's face to her breast saying "Meanwhile, feel free to suck my tits to distract you from the pain."

Lewis grabbed hold of her supple nipple with his mouth and felt the warm flesh dance deliciously along the top of his tongue. He remained ever aware that her sweet, wet vagina hang slightly above his cock which remained rock hard despite, or because of, the damage to his nuts. She moaned as she suckled at her. She arched her back upward staring her beautiful face up into the pale moonlight.

"I was so young when it happened." She said with a dreamy sigh.

Lewis let go of her nipple and asked, "what happened when you were young?"

Mackenzie frowned at him and said, "something that I will never tell a boy. But a few more twists of the torque screw, and I'll be able to tell it to you."

Mackenzie bit her lower lip and looked down between the gap of her breasts at Lewis's rock-hard cock glimmering in the moonlight asked, "do you still want to fuck me?"

Lewis whispered back, "yes."

Mackenzie sighed sadly saying, "that's too bad."

Mackenzie swung her leg up and over Lewis's midsection, leaving her position above him as she reviewed him carefully.

Lewis grimaced and asked, "why did you marry me?"

Mackenzie replied, "I couldn't marry a man. Men are stupid animals which can't be trusted. Women are too much jealousy and drama. You, on the other hand, had an air of promise about you. I've been waiting years to do this to you and I'm starting to feel a bit excited about what might happen next. For now, just keep that clamp on until you no longer want to fuck me." She put a hand on his chest and said in an instructive tone, "If you start to feel the urge for sex, come to me and I'll tighten the screw for you to make those urges go away."

Mackenzie leaned in letting him feel the delicious smoothness of her warm flesh as she hugged Lewis from the side saying, "I'm looking forward to being with you once those urges go away for good." Lewis swallowed hard and wondered how dedicated he was to this relationship. Sure, Mackenzie was his goddess, but his testicles felt as if they would explode. He wasn't sure if they would survive keeping the clamp on much longer. Though, he took one look into Mackenzie's glimmering eyes dancing in the pale moonlight and his stare softened. Who needed testicles when their wife looked like that? Besides, something about this felt like a bizarre, magical breakthrough in their oft strained relationship. Lewis had never seen Mackenzie smile so broadly or look at him in such a loving manner. He smiled back at her. He didn't know how far she was going to take this, but he made up his mind right then and there to trust her no matter what she did to him.

For the first time in a long time, Mackenzie allowed Lewis to stay in bed with her. From time-to-time he would wake up crying in pain and she would shush him back to sleep. At other times, he would wake up and try to press his meaty little cock against her in some vain attempt to obtain sexual pleasure from her body. She would kiss him delicately and lovingly as she twisted ever tighter the clamp around his testicles crushing them with each twist of the screw and ushering him along into a new life without these annoying little organs. She would then hold him tight and lovingly as he cried and whimpered through the pain. Eventually, though, he would fall back asleep as would her laying their in a beautiful little jumble of arms, legs, and torsos. One gorgeous and powerful woman rested alongside a person who was quickly losing rights to make any claim to being a man.

"Have you ever fucked a man before?" Mackenzie asked Lewis from across the breakfast table. Lewis sat a bit uneasily on his now purple and black testicles, which protruded sickly into his undershorts. His long night of pain had done little to assuage his lingering fears of what Mackenzie was doing to him, but he had to admit that he felt less of the maddening desire to fuck her today than what he had felt last night.

"Uhh… no… Mac. I'm not gay." Lewis replied haltingly, not sure how to answer such a bizarre question from his wife.

She giggled and said, "Yeah, of course not. Have you ever thought about it?"

Lewis squinted at her and shook his head, but even as he did so the thought of gay sex entered his mind. He pondered slightly at what it would be like to feel another man's cock filling his mouth. He supposed it wouldn't be too bad, as long as the man was reasonably clean, and his cock didn't taste nasty or something. His thoughts turned to anal sex, and he couldn't really perceive how this could be pleasurable other than perhaps the general sensation of submitting to someone.

"It's kind of magical. You see this big, scary beast, right, I mean a full-sized man is something out of a fucking nightmare, but then you just massage and stroke its cock and suddenly it becomes a pathetic little lap-dog begging for you to let it cum. You get to play with it a bit, tease it, toy with it, make it be your bitch for a while. Eventually, when you get good at fucking men, you can make them do shit for you. Shit they don't even want to do. Shit they can't even believe they are doing until it's too late and they are already doing it. It's truly amazing how easily controlled they are just with a few basic strokes of their cocks."

Lewis cringed internally and asked, "are you talking about what you did to me?"

Mackenzie shook her head and replied, "I would never tell this to a man. You're able to hear this only *because* of what I did to you. Anyhow, I should ask. How are you feeling? Have you lost sensation in your testicles yet? Do you still feel sexual desire?"

Lewis shifted uneasily and replied, "they still hurt."

Mackenzie nodded and said, "let me check them."

Smooth as a panther, Mackenzie got up and stepped around the table before casually dragging the zipper down on Lewis's pants. She was so close that he could feel the warmth of her body and the smell of her breath. She looked intimately into his eyes and gave him a reassuring smile which he returned feeling his cock grow hard at her presence once more.

As she lifted out his manhood she frowned lightly saying, "I see that you're still thinking like a man."

"I'm sorry."

"Don't worry. It isn't anything a few more twists of the screw couldn't fix."

Lewis gulped and shivered, but Mackenzie withdrew the same stubby screwdriver she had used on him last night from her pocket and carefully twisted the screw even tighter. This time, a distinct *crunch* could be heard within Lewis's body, and he wondered if it was loud enough for Mackenzie to hear. No fresh onslaught of pain came, rather a tingling sensation spread strangely through his crotch followed by a sensation of nausea. Lewis couldn't make sense of what he felt, but a part of him started to comprehend that a bit of the critical infrastructure to his body had been lost and the rest now scurried to find how to live on without it.

"Hurt too much?" She asked as he cringed.

"Not really. Much less than it did last night" he replied.

She looked down at his testicles and carefully touched one of them. “Feel that?” She asked him. Lewis shook his head. In truth he felt nothing now, nothing from where his manhood used to be.

She smiled at him and said "good. You're becoming who you were truly meant to be. I think I finally crushed these horrible little things to death and set you free."

"Free to what?" Lewis asked sheepishly.

Mackenzie's phone buzzed and she checked a message on it. A wicked smile spread across her face as she read it.

"Free to help me around the shop."

"But I don't know anything about cars." Lewis protested as he sidestepped around the hydraulic lifts, oil cans, and tools all the while trying to keep up with his wife. For her part, Mackenzie busied herself tightening a bright red and white polka dot scrunchy in her hair while shifting her tight stretchy black shirt down a bit to reveal more of her cleavage. She stopped and turned back to look at Lewis. Her dark eyeliner offset her glittering blue eyes and black hair against her pale face making her almost doll-like, as if she was some 1950's pin-up girl.

She replied, "open your mouth like this" She opened her mouth in an exaggerated "O" shape and Lewis mimicked her, despite the confusion in his mind.

"You're hired." Mackenzie said with a broad smile. She stopped for a moment and looked off dreamily for a moment before whispering, "why am I so excited to do this with you? It feels so weird." She looked at Lewis with a lowered eyebrow of inquisitive nature and asked, "is this what it feels like to fall in love?"

"You weren't in love when we got married?" Lewis asked. Mackenzie scoffed and replied, "I already told you, no. Besides, we eloped to get married by an Elvis impersonator, don't get too bothered about it."

Lewis protested, "but, the Elvis impersonator was your idea."

Mackenzie pursed her lips thoughtfully and replied, "I thought you could give me stability but, well, now I think you can give, or, well, we can be so much more."

Lewis asked, "What's that?"

They entered Mackenzie's waiting room and already two burly naked men stood there. Both gaped at Lewis with just as much shock as he gaped back at them.

A tall, dark-haired man who smelled heavily of cheap cologne spoke up asking, "Wait, Mac? What's he doing here?"

"Team playing, Derrick. Either you and Charles play on a team or you find a new garage."

Mackenzie replied brazenly with a stern look on her face. The other man, younger and with golden hair as well as a somewhat smoother appearance to him, spoke up saying, "that still doesn't explain why he is here."

Mackenzie nodded towards Lewis and said, "my husband will be assisting me today."

Derrick scoffed, "you can't be serious."

Lewis asked "Wait? What?"

Mackenzie gave him a glittering smile and whispered, "I have been unfair with you, having sex with all these studs. Now that you've started to lose your manhood, I can share my studs with you." She stepped in and wrapped an arm around Lewis whispering into his ear as he stared at the two men in disbelief.

She pointed at Derrick who's impressive girthy cock had already been fully erect when they had entered. It had only started to slightly wane at the sight of Lewis. Still, he was a good several inches longer and fuller than Lewis had ever been. She said, "that there is a man's cock. A real cock. Go ahead and take a long look at it."

"There's no way I'm-" Lewis began to sputter, but Mackenzie whispered sweetly into his ear as she pulled him in towards her ample bosom saying, "do it for me."

Lewis stared at Derrick's cock and Derrick began to cringe as it shrunk even more as he grew nervous about the situation.

Mackenzie continued, as she gestured across Derrick's body, saying, "Every part of a man, from his shoulders down to his hips, funnels in towards that beautiful bit of machinery. Throbbing veins, sensitive tip, his power to reproduce, everything is there. It is his command-and-decision center, and you get to be in control of it. You get to step right into his driver's seat and direct waves of pleasure beyond his wildest imagination along their course with your tongue. Afterwards, you can let him take over as he is driven blind with animalistic desire and cannot stop himself from driving the thick shaft deep into your body where you can feel that sensitive little tip dance and play amongst your organs. It is such an incredible feeling." She breathily spoke into Lewis's ear saying, "One that I want to share with you."

Lewis licked his lips as he stared at Derrick's purple tip. Curiosity as to what it would feel like began to fill Lewis with a strange feeling he could not describe. For some reason, the bit of nausea he experienced due to the crushing forces against what little was left of his testicles seemed to heighten this feeling as he started to mentally accept that perhaps he would make a better girl than he ever had a man. Clearly his meager and atrophied cock would be of no comparison to Derrick's monstrous masterpiece, and perhaps it would be best to make no comparison at all rather accepting what

Mackenzie was offering and join his wife in pleasuring men with superior cocks.

"Okay. I trust you. Just tell me what to do." Lewis said.

"Great, go ahead and get your clothes off."

"Are you kidding?" Derrick complained.

Mackenzie snorted and said, "Absolutely not. In fact, I bet the bill of your next repair that my Lewis can give you a better orgasm than I ever did."

Lewis began taking off his shirt as Mackenzie started to strip as well. It felt strange revealing his body, weak and pathetic as it was, in front of men. Meanwhile, his beautiful wife was expertly slipping her gorgeous, curvaceous breasts and hips out from beneath her shirt and workpants. She wore lacey white underwear which contrasted horribly against Lewis's pathetic smiley-face boxers. Lewis made a mental note to look for sexier underwear if he was ever going to cut it at doing sex as a girl.

"I doubt it." Derrick said with a frown.

"Do you want fucked today or not?" Mackenzie asked.

Derrick rolled his eyes and said, "yes."

"Then be open to new experiences. At the very least, do it for me, okay? This is something Lewis and I want to do as a couple."

"For you, Mac, anything." Derrick replied.

As Lewis took off his underwear, Charles pointed in shock, "Holy shit what did you do to his balls?"

"It's part of his transformation. A reminder that he's no longer a man. That's all." Mackenzie replied.

"Take a look at Derrick's balls. Just imagine how nice and warm they will feel pressing softly against your damaged manhood as he shoves his cock into you from behind. Release your ideas about being a man and let him be your man." Lewis did as she instructed and let his imagination follow along her direction. "For the full experience, I want to see if you can cum for Derrick. I want you to get wet and cum like a girl, with your back arched while your body writhes about skewered on top of a man's powerful cock. Do you think you can do that?"

"No." Lewis replied honestly.

"Well, we'll just have to work up to that point. Okay?" Mackenzie replied.

She looped her arm around Lewis and directed him up to the men before saying, "Let's start off with a little taste, first, to show these men that they are your alpha and that their pleasure is all that matters to you. Go ahead and get on your knees. I'll show you what you are to do as I demonstrate on Charles. If, after you get comfortable, you feel like changing it up a bit and trying new things, I'm sure Derrick will appreciate that."

Mackenzie delicately cupped Charles's meaty testicles with her right hand while bringing her pouty lips up to elegantly kiss the smooth, purple head of his trembling cock. She gently licked her exquisite pink tongue right along the slightly bifurcated tip across his urethra. She smirked and remarked, "hmmm… a bit salty. You've been excited for this for a while now."

Lewis's eyes went wide as his hesitation peaked. Inside he conjured a mantra and whispered it to himself saying, "don't think. Just do."

"I'm not sure this is a good id-" Derrick started to say, but he stopped short as Lewis lovingly brought his purple tip into his mouth and suckled at it lightly. To Lewis's delight, Derrick's cock didn't particularly taste bad in any way, rather simply like a bit of flesh with the smallest aftertaste of saltiness to it. Lewis then proceeded to simply do to Derrick what he had always hoped Mackenzie would do to himself. Derrick s gaped as pleasure exploded through his body at the undulation of Lewis's tongue.

At first, Mackenzie giggled lightly, but then her mouth fell open in shock as she watched Lewis continue uninterrupted.

Lewis softly cupped Derrick's balls in his hands and massaged the burly and hairy testicles softly feeling the warmth of Derrick's manhood fill his palm. Lewis let go of his expectations and his self-consciousness and simply decided to enjoy the sensation of plunging himself into Derrick's manhood. Derrick groaned loudly and panting started to come to his mouth as his knees started to weaken. Mackenzie realized that Lewis had no sense of pacing and would soon be getting a mouthful of salty cum before they even had a chance to play further with the studs.

"Hold on." Mackenzie said as she reached over and pulled Lewis back from Derrick. Derrick grumbled "why'd you stop him?" Lewis looked at her in confusion. She smiled with a slight laugh saying, "don't make him cum too fast. We have all morning."

She lovingly licked at Charles's cock saying, "take your time. Let them enjoy the process as much as the finale."

Lewis slowly began again this time delicately kissing his way along the tip of Derrick's swollen shaft. It felt a bit annoying being not only forced onto his knees to suck the cock of another man but then, even in this unusual circumstance, being forced to once again endure the agony of restraint. Lewis had already made peace with the thought that Derrick would cum in his mouth. He actually looked forward to it as the sensation of Derrick's cock pumping would in one sense mean that this bizarre and submissive encounter would be over but, in another sense, indicate that Lewis had succeeded spectacularly. He already imagined Mackenzie congratulating him on pleasuring a man before maybe endeavoring to pleasure Lewis herself.

For her part, Mackenzie did her best to keep up lovingly massaging and kissing her way along Charles's cock. Before briefly stopping to say to Lewis as a reminder, "don't let him cum in your mouth."

Lewis let go and Derrick groaned in annoyance as he called back, "why not? He clearly wants to."

Mackenzie smiled wickedly and replied, "because a real girl would let him cum inside her body. Get on up and get ready for him to penetrate you." Lewis gritted his teeth and stood up. Mackenzie gently guided Charles over to one side of the couch and bent over it forwards presenting her beautifully rounded buttocks and wide-spread hips to him with a sopping wet pussy begging to be penetrated right in front of him.

"Let him take you like this, Lewis. Now is time to let Derrick take control and penetrate you to your core. He'll decide when and how he wants to fill you with cum."

Lewis looked up at Derrick submissively.

"How would you like to fill me with your cum?"

Derrick cocked an eyebrow at him and said, "How about you lay out on the couch so I can watch your wife getting fucked while I fill your ass?" Wordlessly, Lewis lay out sideways on the couch opposite of Mackenzie with his lower half hanging over the arm of the couch opposite from her. Lewis lay on his back and looked up to see Mackenzie leaning over the other arm of the couch. He watched, his view of her upside down, as she cringed and flexed sensually while Charles penetrated her deeply from behind. Lewis smiled at the strangely beautiful sight of his wife fucking another man and a small seed of happiness entered his heart in the thought that the one he loved was truly enjoying this. All he had to do now was let go of any last reservations and let Derrick fuck his ass with his saliva-drenched cock.

Lewis watched intently as Derrick stepped into position and hoisted Lewis's legs up against his chest. Lewis stretched his legs upward and let his right ankle rest on Derrick's broad and powerful shoulder while his left leg lay propped up against the back of the couch. To Lewis's surprise, Derrick ran a loving hand down along the inseam of Lewis's left thigh bringing a gasp of pleasure to Lewis's mouth. "No reason you can't enjoy this too." Derrick said as he wrapped his warm, strong fingers around Lewis's tiny cock. He massaged Lewis's relatively small purple head with his broad thumb and slightly and gave a winning smile. "It's so small." Derrick murmured in a complimentary and loving fashion. Lewis started to apologize but Derrick continued "You know. I actually kind of like your little cock. It's cute." In that instant, Lewis realized what women see in men. That winning blend of care and confidence made Lewis want to stay there forever submitting his body over to Derrick for his pleasure. Lewis whispered back, "thank you."

Derrick continued dropping his hands bringing them to grasp either side of Lewis's butt-cheeks. Lewis gritted his teeth as he felt Derrick gently pry him open with his thumbs and a sense of ticklish fear emanated from his loins as Lewis felt incredibly vulnerable in that moment. Derrick pressed his hips slowly forward and Lewis felt the throbbing hot tip of Derrick's manhood begin to penetrate his ass. A bit of pain came as Lewis's ass found itself beginning to stretch in ways it had not stretched before. Lewis cringed with a wincing gasp.

"Shhh… I'll go slow." Derrick whispered down to him. Lewis nodded as he felt the constant, growing pressure within his buttock forcing him upward. He became aware of hot breath just across his forehead and looked up one again to see Mackenzie now collapsed on her elbows as Charles's continued to pound her from behind.

They had already entered a nearly dance-like rhythm of thrusts and returns and she alternated between moaning and whimpering as her face contorted with ultimate pleasure.

Lewis looked down at Derrick slowly and patiently filling his ass with his cock. It seemed like his cock went on forever and Lewis definitely began to feel his insides stretch and warp to make room for it. Derrick's constant, slow thrusting pressure inched his cock into Lewis bit-by-bit forcing Lewis's weak body to accept the presence of the alpha cock within it. Lewis felt bad at making Derrick wait to really do anything fun, so he whispered, "I'm sorry that I'm not really a girl for you."

Derrick gave him a smile and continued pressing inside saying, "that's okay. I can't believe how tight you feel. You're much tighter than your wife and your insides feel incredible." Lewis smiled, but his smile disappeared as Derrick shoved himself in the rest of the way bridging the last few inches all at once making Lewis's eyes nearly bug out of his head. A strange, itchy painful sensation blended with an incredible feeling of 'fullness' as if his abdomen had more inside it than what it was meant to contain, filled Lewis's body.

Lewis focused his mind on the warm sensation of Derrick's abdomen gently cupping his dead balls and Derrick's testicles softly pressed against Lewis's butt cheeks. Lewis breathed through the pain. He had done it. He had taken a man fully inside himself, and not just any man, a well-hung man with an impressively sized cock.

"Oh, oh, okay. I'll just stay here for a moment until you adjust." Derrick said reassuringly.

"Thank you. Just give me a second. I feel my ass stretching out for you, but it needs a bit of time." Derrick smiled and said "No worries. How about you have a little fun while we wait." Derrick grabbed up Lewis's cock in his hand again and gently caressed the tip of it bringing shivers across Lewis's body. The erotic blend of fullness within his ass and massage across his cock made Lewis arc backwards. To his surprise, a pair of female lips came into his view as Mackenzie kissed him passionately from above while Charles still fervently rammed her from behind making her bob up and down slightly during the kiss.

"Feels good to have a strong man's cock inside you, doesn't it?" Mackenzie asked as she released the kiss. Lewis nodded shyly.

Derrick ran his fingers along Lewis's cock making him moan softly and then began pulling out and thrusting back into Lewis's ass making him groan in a pleasure he had never experienced before.

Derrick called out to Charles saying, "Charles, slow up."

"Why?" Charles asked nearly built up to spraying hot sticky cum all over the inside of Mackenzie.

A sinister little smile came over Derrick's face as he said, "they're a married couple. We should make them cum at the same time."

Charles slowed his pace slightly as Mackenzie protested softly, "no fair."

Derrick continued his thrusts growing ever more ambitious with each one as he went. Throughout this, he held onto Lewis's cock as if it was a handle to brace himself against for fucking Lewis's ass and massaged it with his thumb watching a small droplet of watery pre-cum form at Lewis's tip. Derrick chuckled softly saying, "don't get your panties in a twist, Mac, I bet your husband here is going to be cumming pretty damn soon. Actually, I wander what his tight ass will feel like while he's cumming. Probably pretty damn hot based on how it feels now."

Derrick continued his thrusts and playing with Lewis's small cock while Charles began once again ramming Mackenzie deep inside stretching out the sensitive walls of her vagina. Mackenzie and Lewis looked at one another with each one's head upside down to the other one. A smile passed between them. They did the only thing they could do in that moment and kissed each other as the burly studs continued fucking both of them.

Lewis released the kiss first as he could with-hold his orgasm no longer. He groaned loudly with a whimpering little scream at the end as his small cock burst forth little jets of watery, useless cum all across his chest and belly. Derrick groaned as he continued thrusting his cock deep in Lewis's ass. "Good boy, good little boy… just like I thought, my nice thick cock in your ass and my hand around your cock made you cum in no time. It's so fucking sweet to feel your ass flexing and tightening around my cock as you cum."

Just as Derrick finished saying this, Mackenzie screamed in ecstasy as Charles reached a fevered pitch with his thrusts and groaned loudly as the two of them collapsed forward across the couch arm.

Lewis looked down at Derrick and smiled coyly as he huffed out, "your turn."

Lewis flexed his leg and brought his ankle around behind Derrick's buttocks pulling the burly man in closer to him feeling his cock stretch out his ass even further. Lewis leaned back and gritted his teeth feeling incredible pain in his intestines which he ignored. Lewis pushed away thoughts of doubt and trepidation and only focused on the rising sense of accomplishment which came with Derrick's haggard breath and the surreal swell of his cock growing even harder within Lewis. Lewis flexed his leg in a fast tempo drawing Derrick in deeper and faster. "Go ahead. Release your cum deep inside me. I want to have it as a little souvenir to remember you by" Lewis whispered as he felt the alpha male begin to grow week in his knees. It barely took two more pumps for Derrick to lose it and nearly howl out in ecstasy as Lewis felt some hot, wet explosion fill his bowels. Lewis blinked in surprise as Derrick toppled over and collapsed across Lewis's midsection groaning in pleasure. Lewis smiled and playfully tussled Derrick's hair as it lay on his chest with a smug little look filling his face. A strange sense of accomplishment filled his heart, one he had never sensed before during those dark, cold, lonely nights of frustration and despair that he had felt as a sub-par man. Lewis ran his fingers on down and across Derrick's muscular shoulders. Derrick was too exhausted by his thrusting to even react to this touch, but Lewis continued to caress him lovingly. Lewis marveled that, had it been a fistfight or any kind of contest, there would be no way he could defeat such a powerful man. Here, however, Lewis had accomplished incredible things with Derrick's body and somehow Lewis had the sense that Derrick would now take care of him and maybe even love him for the sex that they had shared. Lewis shook his head to break away from this fantasy. He leaned his head back and felt lithe fingers grab around his face pulling him towards the face of his wife who kissed him passionately as she whispered, "I have never loved you more than I do right now."

"You were absolutely incredible!" Mackenzie gushed at Lewis over supper that night. He smiled coyly as he pressed a fork full of broccoli into his mouth. He chewed it up and swallowed it down saying, "for what it's worth, I never knew I could do that." Mackenzie nodded saying, "you're an absolute natural." He picked up another forkful of food and put it in her mouth as she sat perched on his lap. Ever since Charles and Derrick, she had hardly left his side. She had demanded he stay with her for the rather less sexual parts of her day which involved legitimate automobile work. At even the slightest passing opportunity, she would plant wet, warm, loving kisses on his face. She would drag him in close for delicious make-out sessions.

Strangely, however, none of these actions served to make Lewis hard anymore. Instead, however, the hot, lush body of his wife, her sensual wet lips, her softly rounded breasts felt more friendly and familiar than desirous. Almost as if Lewis was now her best friend or perhaps sister or something.

"Is it always like that, when a man takes you?" Lewis asked. Mackenzie looked down sadly and replied "not really. Sometimes, men are mean about it. Sometimes they hurt you. I think you can appreciate how scary that can be. Being at the mercy of someone much larger and stronger than yourself."

Lewis imagined if Derrick had forcibly raped him instead of the measured, consensual sex they had shared. He shivered lightly and said, "that must absolutely terrifying."

Mackenzie nodded and said, "I used to think that's the way all men had sex. It's like getting beaten up by a bully. He takes what he wants from you then leaves you crying. Of course, that was back when I was little and…" she stared down sadly. Lewis gave her a reassuring hug and said "if you're not ready to talk about it. It's okay."

Mackenzie snorted and replied, "it's been almost twenty years. If I'm not ready to talk about it now, I never will be. I could never tell a man. Even the nice ones just have some sex and then leave, you know. You can't really ever trust a man because, deep down inside, they all want to have sex with your body, and they will say and do whatever it takes to get it." She looked apprehensively at Lewis and asked, "do you still want to have sex with my body?"

Lewis considered how far he had come on this topic in the last twenty-four hours. If she had sat in his lap yesterday, he would have barely been able to control himself. Now, however, he almost kind of hoped she would invite Derrick back for round two more so than take him herself. He replied, "not now. It's not that I don't like you. I feel closer to you now than I ever have before. It's just that I don't feel like I'm a man who should take a woman at all."

Mackenzie smiled and said, "I knew the clamp would work. Whatever testosterone your balls were producing before is now completely gone as we've successfully crushed your balls to death. Since you don't want my body anymore, I will explain. When I was a little girl, my uncle would use me. I wouldn't even call it sex. He just took what he wanted from me and left me crying in pain and in shame."

"I'm so sorry to hear that." Lewis replied.

Mackenzie sighed and said, "eventually I couldn't hide it anymore and I told my parents. Police arrested him and my dad said he no longer had a brother. You would think knowing my uncle would never see the light of day again would bring me peace, but it didn't. Weirdly, the only thing that brought me a sense of solace and protection was when I was fucking. I suppose it was because the only time my uncle wasn't beating me was when he was inside me and so I just associated having a man inside me with a sense of safety. I don't feel safe unless a man is inside me, but I know the sick desires all men hold so, once they are done, I just send them on their way. I guess that's why I act the way I act."

Lewis considered this and asked, "That makes sense for them. But I still don't understand why you married me."

Mackenzie sighed and replied, "because you are the exact opposite of my uncle in every way. I suppose part of me held out hope for you to complete this metamorphosis even before our wedding night."

Lewis twisted his lips and asked, "so you were planning to castrate me when we first met?"

Mackenzie looked off dreamily saying, "it was all I could think about, even though I didn't have the guts to do it until just recently. I doubt I am alone in saying that all women dream of having a gelded husband."

The shop bell rang, and they both looked at it in attention. Mackenzie chuckled saying "our evening entertainment has arrived." Lewis asked, "really?" Mackenzie nodded saying, "Steve Mira, he's every bit of nine-inches long. Think you can handle it?" Lewis chuckled and replied, "well I suppose a man's gotta do the man that he's gotta do."

The Practice Sissy

"I just can't seem to work up the nerve to talk to her."

Jeremiah complained as we sat playing video games together in my room. He was whipping my butt again, but I didn't really mind. Mostly he played against me just for practice to get better for the online tournaments he would sometimes enter. As my side of the screen turned crimson red and the words "You are dead." blared across it. I put down my controller and stretched my legs a bit.

"Why are you nervous? It's just Jill." I replied, with a bit more disdain in my voice than what I had intended. Jeremiah looked over at me and smiled with a slight grimace. I watched as he adjusted his body a bit on one of my bean bag chairs. I contemplated the old lies told to us in middle school health about how puberty would make us boys tall and strong. We were all dweeby little kids back then, but somehow my puberty skipped right over me and hit my best friend Jeremiah twice. There could be no other explanation for how he grew to be six-foot four and well over two hundred pounds of muscle while I still hung around in junior sized clothing barely breaking five-foot five and a hundred fifty pounds on a good day. Naturally, Jeremiah's size put him on the basketball team as center while, for me, once the team started making cuts, I was the first to go. Despite this, I wasn't angry at Jeremiah. He was still my best friend even as we went from evenly matched to looking like a little kid and grown man, respectively, despite being the same age.

"It's not easy for me to talk to girls like it is for you, Jordan. You know how I get all mush-mouthed around one of them. For you, it just seems so easy."

I took this in thoughtfully. He did have a point, of course. Most girls' hearts sank in terror the moment they had to crane their necks up to look up and Jeremiah. For me, however, I was practically treated like the sister they never had. I suppose being small and non-threatening has some advantages in making friends with girls, but none had ever contemplated going any further than the dreaded friend-zone with me. Because of this, I would hardly consider myself a romantic expert.

What bugged me wasn't that Jeremiah was after a girl, it was that he was wasting his time on Jill. I knew Jeremiah could do better than horse-faced Jill. He could easily get Casey or Alexis, who I knew from the paparazzi had been staring at his bulge during ball practice. Still, he had a point in that I haven't seen him even speak to a girl since second grade. Even though I sat trapped on the sidelines of being a friend, it wasn't like silent stares were going to get Jeremiah a girlfriend any faster.

"Well, I might be able to help you." I said back to him.

"You got advice?" He asked, hopefully.

I opened my mouth and then closed it furrowing my brow saying, "not really, no. I mean, I talk with girls all the time, but it's not like I'm picking them up. If anything, I should say I know more about what it's like for girls to be girls than how to get one to be my girlfriend."

"Ah, nuts. You know the dance was coming up and I was hoping to ask Jill out to it. Every time I see her it's like my mouth locks up or some shit. Hell, it's like that for every girl. Weird, I have no problem throwing in a body-check against that chungus-looking kid from Anderson Central grabbing a rebound. But, with a girl, It's like my mind just stops." Jeremiah explained.

I wanted to help my friend out and I thought through what I could do. Jeremiah frowned thoughtfully. I let my eyes wander along his massive, muscular frame finding it hard to believe he would be afraid of anything, much less a girl. He seemed to be bursting out from his soft polyester gym shorts and NBA logo bearing T-shirt. My eyes trailed along the softly mounded bulge at his crotch longer than I wanted them to.

“But maybe I could help you practice?” I said.

“Huh?” Jeremiah asked in confusion.

"Well, just pretend I'm a girl and then ask me to the dance?"

At this, Jeremiah started laughing and replied, "Jordan, you're obviously a dude."

An idea sprang into my mind and my eyes lit up as I said, "what if I dress up a bit to help you with your nerves?"

"Dress up?" He asked giving me an odd stare.

I nodded across the hall to my sister's empty room saying, "my sis has everything I would need. Even some wigs from when she does cosplay. She's having a sleep-over at a friend's house so it's not like she'll need any of it now. I'll just return it all after you get over your jitters. Okay?"

"You would seriously dress like Jill for me?" Jeremiah asked blinking in surprise.

I crinkled up my nose and replied, "No, not Jill. I have standards. If I'm going to dress like a girl, it's going to be Alexis."

Jeremiah chuckled saying, "Alexis? I thought she was going out with Steve."

I shook my head and said "no, they broke up last month. The word on the street is that Alexis is interested in you." Jeremiah gestured at me and asked, "how did you know that?"

I shrugged and replied, "I talk to girls."

Jeremiah flung his head back and made a groaning sound, "back to my problem. It feels like I got cotton in my mouth whenever I'm around a girl."

I said, "Well, what do you think of Alexis?"

Jeremiah smirked and said, "hottest girl in the school with that gorgeous tight little body of hers and those cute little dimples. God, I'm barely able to keep the fucking ball on the court with her prancing around on the sideline in that little cheerleader outfit. Any guy with a fucking pulse would want a piece of that sweet ass. Yeah, I would love to take Alexis, but if I can't even work up the nerve to talk to Jill, there's no way I can do so for Alexis."

I gestured towards myself and said, "well if it's just nerves then I can help you with that. It's not like you go into a game against Springfield Central first thing in the season. You practice at basketball you practice for a girl. I can help you practice at talking to a girl. It's just me, dude. It's not like you're going to hurt my feelings or anything."

Jeremiah looked up at me with a vague recognition of hope. I suppose my parallel between girls and basketball clicked in his mind. "You would do that for me?" He asked.

I nodded.

"Why?" he asked with earnest curiosity in his voice.

"I don't want you moping around all school year like a sad sack." I blurted out with a laugh before noticing he didn't find this funny, and I quelled my laughter continuing, "I just want my friend to be happy."

Jeremiah smiled at me and said, "dude, you are literally the best. Okay. Let's do it but, if anyone asks, this never happened. God knows what the paparazzi will do if they found out I had my buddy dress up like a girl just so I could get used to talking to one."

I chuckled and replied, "why would I tell anyone about this?

Jeremiah seemed to visibly relax at these words as he continued, "of course. Man, I owe you one for this."

I stood up and said, "I'll go get ready. This will take a bit of time but I'm going to do my best to bring the experience to life."

I lay a hand on his muscular arm. I paused for a moment, feeling his strong, sure pulse beating just beneath the surface of his warm skin. A strange desire to touch him more filled me and I began to wonder if I had an ulterior motive for offering up myself to 'practice' on that was so secretive I could not even admit it to myself. A part of me somehow wanted his muscular arm. I wanted to feel it wrapped around me. I wanted it to put my body where he wanted it to go. I wanted to submit myself to his desire.

He looked up at me with his large, brown eyes and I snapped out of my thoughts. I continued "when I get back, just think of me like I am Alexis, we're at school, you're asking me out. I'll do my best to stay in the role. Got it?"

Jeremiah reached up and ran his burly hands through his curly hair blowing out a nervous sigh before replying, "got it. Thanks so much for this."

It felt strange sneaking out from my own room and slipping into my sisters. I did my best to pad my footfalls, so my parents wouldn't hear me in her room. Behind me sat the masculine world of movie posters, rap music, and video games. I now stepped into my older sister's prissy pink palace complete with hello kitty bed spread, makeup table, and a closet full of thin, girly clothes. She also had her own built-in bathroom since her room had technically been the master bedroom when we bought the house. This combined with her passion for cosplay and my lack of growth leaving me about her size meant I had everything I needed to transfigure myself however girly I wanted to look.

I knew it wouldn't quite be a linear path turning myself into Alexis, but I knew I had to start somewhere...

But where?

My mind tore in conflict as I contemplated how 'far' I would go to become Alexis for Jeremiah. My heart quivered as I pictured him standing in front of me desperately blurting out awkward small-talk or whatever.

Of course, with me…

…he would succeed.

I mean, of course he would succeed. My 'Alexis' would agree to go out with him no matter how mush-mouthed he was. I desperately needed to build up his confidence for her and a strange thought crossed my mind as my lower lip began to quiver.

Alexis owed *me* for this, big time.

I imagined what it would be like to be her, so small, so delicate, so coddled within the massive grip of Jeremiah experiencing passion and yearning the likes of which would secure for her such love and support beyond her wildest imagination. I groaned lightly as I imagined what it would be like to be her. I would lay my tight little body back and stretch out my legs invitingly as burly Jerome pressed his cock deep inside making my eyes roll back into my head with overwhelming sensation of him invading and filling every part of me. I would lay there in passion as he claimed my lithe little body as his own.

I clenched my teeth as I wondered if even Alexis was good enough to deserve such amazing treatment.

Hot, yes, but she was kind of stuck up too and…

I shook my head to chase away the darkening thoughts.

I was being a douchebag leaving my buddy hanging. Alexis was what I promised him, and Alexis is what he was going to get. My heart grew set on my next course of action. I would go all the way for Jeremiah. Even if that prissy little 'real-Alexis' didn't appreciate what he was giving her, I would do *my* part to be the best 'fake-Alexis' he could possible experience.

I proceeded to the bathroom whispering to myself, "my Alexis is going to shave her legs for him."

It felt strange, quietly running the warm water over my sister's razor before lathering some of her fruity-smelling shave cream onto my legs and running the blade over them. It did, however, definitely put me into a more effeminate mood than I had ever experienced before in my life. I had always experienced these things as something I 'saw' or 'smelled' from a distance on someone else but now I was experiencing shaved legs for myself, and I must admit…

One star…do not recommend.

I clumsily nicked myself a few times before finally getting smart and padding out into the hallway to grab one of my facial razors from the closet before returning to complete my task. With a newfound appreciation for how superior the design of a man's flexible facial razor is compared to its stiff-bladed, shitty female counterpart and also for how superior the lathering capabilities of female shave cream is to its flat and musky male counterpart, I swept my legs clean of unwanted hair. The sensation left me feeling like I had taken off my legs and affixed girl ones on in their place. Conflict filled my mind once more as I brought the blade up now to my buttocks and crotch. As I saw my sagging balls and soft cock drooping lightly beneath my contemplative blade I half pondered if I could just take them off and replace them with a proper vagina so I could go back in and actually 'be' Alexis for him. Nothing of that sort would be accomplished without major and permanent surgery, however I did want to prepare my body for Jeremiah in whatever way I possibly could. I proceeded to lather and shave my way across not only my balls and crotch but up the back of my buttocks, across my chest, and even my armpits. Mercifully, a lack of full puberty left me significantly less hairy than most boys my age. This made this feat even possible, and I smiled as

I ran my fingers appreciatively over my newly smooth skin under the gentle spray of my sister's very-slightly turned-on shower. I padded dry with one of her towels and stepped back out into her room. I quietly padded over to her dresser opening it revealing row after row of underwear. I snorted thinking that the real Alexis would just wear cheap cotton panties or some crap to the dance. She would probably squander the opportunity to impress him with a visual feast of her body encased in something delicate and beautiful.

Jeremiah deserved better than that.

"My Alexis will wear lingerie for Jeremiah." I muttered to myself as I pawed through trying to pick out what lingerie I thought Jeremiah would like best. I finally settled on a pair of red, lacey panties which bore a convenient opaque panel in the front with an open-mesh lacey rear that proudly displayed the delicate and sensual skin encased within. The panel was what really cinched it for me and as I slid them on over my shaved legs a strange tingle went up my spine. A bizarre, almost nauseous feeling replaced that tingle tickling a sensation deep within my belly as I delicately tucked my little cock and balls into the opaque panel hiding these unwanted organs from view save for a faint hump where they resided. "Out of sight, out of mind." I whispered to myself.

Although I didn't technically have any breasts to warrant a bra, Alexis didn't have much of these either. Alexis's attraction rested mainly in her hips while her top half remained more slimly athletic than voluptuous. I would, however, still put on a bra because it would be necessary to complete the transition. Picking through my options, I found a cute little red lacey bra that I felt confident my parents were unaware of my sister having. I slid it on and spent an inordinate amount of time trying to clasp it in the back. "How do girls do this?" I muttered to myself as I fumbled about with the clip before finally figuring out that it needed to slide past and then back onto the hooks. It felt bizarrely natural and surprisingly supportive. I had no chest to fill out even the menial A-cups, such as they were, but they did provide a pleasant visual contrast. I reviewed myself in my sister's mirror and my jaw dropped in shock. I sensually stuck out a hip and winked then gasped at my own reflect.

I was already starting to feel intimidated by the sensual girl staring back at me.

I wasn't Alexis yet but, even in just a set of lingerie and with a shaved body, I could already start to pass as one of those pixie girls. I smiled and adopted a few different poses pondering which one Jeremiah would like best. My mind slowly started drifting through how much he would like them as the memory of fantasies that bespelled me while holding onto his beefy arm began to clutter my brain. I took a deep breath to steady myself.

"You're doing this so he can get a date with Alexis, remember?" I spoke to myself as the thoughts of helping the girl who didn't really talk to me that much started to fade in my mind.

I turned back to my sister's outfits and said, "Alexis, Alexis, what would Alexis wear?" I picked through these carefully. Obviously, Alexis was classically affiliated with a cheerleader outfit, but that felt a bit too school-official and surely wouldn't be anything she would wear to a dance or formal event. At the same time, was I trying to replicate Alexis at the dance or at school? The looks would be completely different. I looked down at my lingerie and decided that I might try to split the difference but hedge a bit on 'dance' attire with less respect for compliance to school dress code than real Alexis would exercise (and she pushed that boundary every day).

"If I'm going to be Alexis, I'm going to look damn good while being her too" I spoke thoughtfully as I sifted through my options. I had already pushed the 'commit' button when I tucked my cock into red lingerie. I wasn't going to hold back on the sex-appeal now. I felt grateful that my sister had taught me a bit about fashion, even if I did feel slightly out of my league. I found a red, sweetheart-cut blouse and slid it on feeling grateful that I was still small enough for it to fit. I paired this with a black miniskirt whose lower hem terminated just barely in compliance with the notorious school 'finger-tip' test. I reviewed myself in the mirror turning about to check my own ass. What little bit I did have seemed well accentuated by the tight clothing such that I truly looked a bit effeminate. I hemmed and hawed a bit about the 'realism' of Alexis wearing this feeling it hedged significantly more on the side of dance and was something she would not wear at school. I licked my lips and looked over my shoulder checking out my own ass as I whispered, "I shouldn't worry about how the real Alexis dresses. This is how my Alexis dresses." I did a little spin and raised my arms in a delicate pose smiling as the dress cut and bra gave me a convincing illusion of breasts. I continued "my Alexis dresses sexy for Jeremiah because she wants him to see her. She wants him to enjoy staring at her lithe little body. She relishes getting up every day and putting on something sexy knowing he'll enjoy looking at her in it later."

I felt giddy.

The hair was easy as my sister already had black, shoulder-length curly-haired wig. I put it on and then played around with a few different styles for the hair before deciding to tie it back in a simple ponytail of curls which cascaded like a waterfall down the back of my neck the way Alexis almost always had her hair. I marveled at how itchy this felt and wondered how girls handled having such an experience all the time. Next came makeup and my sister's lessons proved to be incredibly valuable as I sat there at her vanity mirror applying concealer and foundation to smooth out my sharp, masculine appearance, and continued with blush, eyeliner, and mascara to highlight the width between my eyes for heightened effeminate beauty. My heart raced as I went through this process thinking about how Jeremiah would soon see me wearing all this and I fantasized about his reaction. As a final step, I grabbed up a stick of my sister's bright-red lipstick and painted on supple, delicious lips onto my face.

I stared into the mirror.

Alexis stared back at me.

No… not completely.

I hadn't quite captured the stuck-up cheerleader. Rather, I had something even better. The real Alexis would lack the guts to go through with dressing this way, but my Alexis knew no such fears and boundaries. My Alexis only dressing for the benefit of Jeremiah. As such, I felt confident that any hot-blooded man with a pulse would stare gape-jawed at me dressed and made up such as I was and this feeling bolstered confidence within me.

I played there for a while turning my head to one side or another while pouting sensually. I practiced languid stares and dropped my jaw in feigned shock while fluttering my eyes coyly. I spoke, "Hi Jeremiah, how's the game treating you?" I coughed and adjusted my voice. Mercifully, along with my lack of height and weight, I had scarcely developed any significant depth to my voice such that I did not have to conjure up a ridiculous falsetto to match her tone. I simply slide up into the alto clef from my normal tenor. After a few more practice runs, I felt confident that, although I had not nailed all her mannerisms, I did present an incredible facsimile of a gorgeous girl based on Alexis. I shivered lightly in anticipation pondering how Jeremiah would react to seeing me like this. Fantasies played out in my mind leaving me with the disturbing question of what, exactly, I was hoping for happening deep down at my core. My small, quivering body trembled at the thought of what Jeremiah might do to it when he saw me like this. I clutched my hands to my chest and then looked down to them.

I was already starting to act like a girl, clutching at my 'pearls' and whimpering submissively. I whispered a silent prayer to no god in particular that, whatever happened, Jeremiah would feel better afterwards. I just wanted to see him happy so badly.

To prevent any incriminating clacking sounds, I carried my sister's strappy black leather sandals in my hand across the hall and slipped them on just outside my own bedroom door. My heart pounded loud in my chest with a mixture of fear and anticipation. My mind whirred as I couldn't believe what I was doing. "You can do this." I whispered to myself. I forced my trembling hand up and pushed my bedroom door open. I quietly slipped inside dressed as a girl for the benefit of my friend.

Jeremiah looked up at me from the video game console and his jaw fell open. He rose to his feet and stammered stepping back a few steps, "Alexis?"

I smiled back at him sweetly.

He trembled and then squinted.

I couldn't believe it.

At first, I thought he was just saying the name of my muse, but now I saw he legitimately thought that I was Alexis somehow magically teleported into my house.

I must have done better than I thought.

I pondered my options very briefly. I considered pulling off the wig and reminding him it's just me but being this close to Jeremiah and so convincingly girlish I couldn't resist my own desires. I spun around lightly letting him see me from all angles before returning with a smile asking, "do you like?"

He began panting as his eyes went wide. His mouth opened but no words came out. I could see his growing fear and so I quickly closed distance and placed my small hand on his warm arm and said reassuringly to him "Jeremiah, it's okay. It's still me, on the inside of all of this…" I gestured across my body saying "…Jordan. I'm your friend. you're not going to offend or anger me. Okay?"

Slowly Jeremiah nodded. He clasped a warm hand across the top of my own and looked down at our hands crossed over on his arm. I could tell that he felt it too. Holding his hand just seemed so…

Natural.

I felt this was where I was meant to be. Cheated by biology into a small body it was only right for me to be here, submissively fulfilling the pleasures of an alpha male like Jeremiah. For his part, I could see in his eyes the confused realities between "girl" and "best friend dressed as a girl" blend and warp within him.

He finally found his voice as he whispered, "Holy shit! Jordan. I thought you would just throw on some skinny jeans or something." I smiled up at him warmly feeling some effeminate people-pleaser mood passing through me. He continued "You… you seriously look like a girl. I mean, exactly like Alexis even. I don't know what to say."

"That's okay. Let's pretend we're at school."

Jeremiah chuckled, "Principal Stonesill would definitely not allow that outfit at school."

"just pretend. Okay?"

Jeremiah nodded.

I grabbed up a textbook and sat down at my desk pretending to read it. After a few moments, nothing happened. I cast my gaze at Jeremiah and silently beckoned for him to come over with my fingers.

"Hey, Alexis."

"Hi Jeremiah." I said copying the sing-song voice Alexis uses when someone has something she wants.

"Come on, dude. She isn't going to be that easy." Jeremiah protested breaking character.

"What are you talking about?" I replied, still keeping my voice in a higher register.

Shockingly, this cowed Jeremiah a bit as he stammered, "I uhh… sorry, nothing."

"Okay. Did you, like, want to ask me something or whatever?" I tried my best to pepper in some of Alexis's annoying mannerisms

He stared at me trembling for a second.

"Would you go out to the Spring Formal with me?" He asked.

I don't know why my heart leaped out of my chest at those words.

Seriously…

Somehow hearing a boy ask you out clearly has some kind of vicarious thrill, even if he's pretending to ask a girl you're dressed as out for nothing but practice.

"I would love to." I replied with a gasping smile.

"Great, okay, bye" Jeremiah blubbered out.

"Wait?" I retorted.

"What?"

"When should I expect you to pick me up?"

"Uhh…"

I wanted to break character but opted instead to simply help him out 'as' Alexis. "Well, you know, the dance is like at seven thirty so pick me up at six?"

"Six?" Jeremiah asked incredulously.

I rolled my eyes but held character, "Well, of course, sweet boy. I would like to go out and eat with you beforehand."

"Alexis wouldn't…" Jeremiah protested.

I let my glare do the talking.

"I'll come around your place at six."

"Great, and when you're talking to the real Alexis, make sure you start off with this rather than making her wheedle it out of you." I replied, still holding Alexis's voice.

"Got it, offer to pick her up at six."

"Do you want to try again?" I asked.

"Could we?"

I nodded and went back to pretending to read the book. I felt surreally vulnerable as he stepped in closer this time. Rather than helping him, I let Jeremiah initiate the conversation this time.

"Hey, uh, Alexis."

"Mmm…" I whimpered lightly as I turned to face him. He towered over me standing extremely close. I would have corrected him on this, but some part of looking up at him across his warm, powerful body made my will feel weak and helpless. I prayed he would take charge of the situation because my mind grew lost in the fantasy of being Alexis sitting this close to the impressive bulge at his crotch… close enough to reach out and touch it… or perhaps… taste it. I didn't have time to shake my head to chase away these thoughts overwhelming my brain forcing me to forget that I was a boy too before he said, "the spring dance is coming up and I wanted to know if you would like to go with me."

A familiar flutter came to my heart.

I smiled and breathily "yes." I didn't even have to force my voice into a higher register. It naturally adopted this tone as I succumbed into my desire to be a girl in that moment sitting there so close to his masculinity.

"Great, I'll pick you up around six and take you to La Fresca beforehand?"

I nodded meekly and licked my lips absentmindedly as I stared up at him saying, "that, would be wonderful. Yes. I'll see you at six."

"Great, well, I got to get to class but I'll see you then." He said as he pretended to step away.

"Yes. Of course." I blubbered mindlessly in Alexis's voice.

"Can we do dinner?" Jeremiah asked.

I blinked at him in confusion.

"You want to eat, now? It's like three in the afternoon." I stammered.

"No, I mean, practice dinner... like what I should…" Jeremiah stumbled over his words.

"Oh, as Alexis. Of course." I replied. I pushed away notebooks from my desk and Jeremiah turned it around for us forming an impromptu table. We slid in some chairs, and I ripped out a few pieces of notebook paper scrawling the words "FOOD" on each and putting them down in front of us. Jeremiah laid out some pens as "utensils" and I propped up a desk lamp to serve as an impromptu candle. I then stepped over to the light switch feeling conscientious of my noisy shoes, even though my parents would be more likely situated beneath my sister's room than my own. As I turned off my room lights, I glanced back at Jeremiah and pursed my lips.

He was totally staring at my ass.

Sure, he looked away as soon as I turned back, but my freshly shaved legs swaying beneath the borrowed skirt teetering on top of my sister's black sandals apparently lent enough sexuality to my body to attract his gaze. I should have been disgusted, but I was rather flattered and blushed lightly as I stepped back over to the table with a smile knowing that I had dressed so convincingly as Alexis that Jeremiah was gaining some sexual pleasure just by looking at me. I felt glad I could do that for my friend and, with my newfound appreciation for just how hard girls have to work to look like this, a sense of accomplishment washed over me with the knowledge that I had seduced such a powerful male into staring at my ass.

I stepped over to my seat and stared at him.

"What?" he asked.

I gestured towards the chair.

"I don't get it."

"A gentleman would pull a chair out for a girl he likes." I said in a higher voice.

"Oh, shit, yeah...." Jeremiah replied as he rushed around my desk to pull back the chair. I daintily alighted upon it demurely squeezing my knees together as he pushed it back in.

"I keep screwing this stuff up." Jeremiah grumbled as he returned to his seat.

"That's why you get to practice with training Alexis before you face the real one." I said as I folded the paper in front of me in half and held it like it was a menu pretending to review my options.

"Training Alexis?" Jeremiah replied.

I looked over the menu and nodded with a smile.

Jeremiah blew out a sigh saying, "Training Alexis… takes too long to say. How about I call you Lexi? You know, her nickname."

I beamed "Lexi, I like it."

"Great, I could never repay you for this, man."

"Maybe not but you could tell me what is good to eat here." I replied reviewing the menu.

"I uhh… don't know."

I nodded over to his phone saying, "look it up."

He looked at me and back at the phone a few times before reaching over and grabbing it to troll reviews for La Fresca.

"It would be rude to check the internet when you are in the presence of Alexis but you're not going to offend Lexi. What does it say?"

"Famous for their shrimp salad as well as pork marinade." Jeremiah replied reading from his screen.

"Brilliant. Memorize that so you have it known for Alexis for later. Now, we've ordered our food and now we're waiting for it to arrive. Is there anything you want to learn about me?"

Jeremiah squinted "Learn about you?"

I shrugged and said "it's a date. You get to know each other. A good chance to ask about Alexis's family, schoolwork, dreams, aspirations, plans…"

"Do you have any brothers?" I asked Jeremiah.

"Dude you already know about my annoying little brother." He protested.

I gestured in the air saying "No, Jeremiah, your little brother is still in intermediary school, so real Alexis wouldn't know him. What's he like?"

Jeremiah went through discussing his little brother before, at my promptings, he moved on to talk about other aspects of his life finishing off by telling me about his friend Jordan who is incredibly helpful. I smirked at this and encouraged him to ask 'Lexi' about her homelife. I filled in from what I did know about Alexis and made up the rest as we came to bond over our mutual love of football and disdain for Algebra. I never dropped Lexi's voice finding it almost easier to keep my girlish voice rather than try to swap back and forth between it and my own. Eventually the conversation turned to hopes and dreams as our 'food' arrived and we pretended to eat it with the pen-utensils. I felt his warm, hairy leg lightly touch my own shaved leg and then pull away in fear for a moment as I glanced at him knowingly. He then slowly put his leg back letting me feel the sensual masculinity of his body sweetly caressed against my own freshly shaved leg. I continued to eat with a coy smile that gave him implicit permission to touch me as we made our way through dinner.

After we shared one desert with two spoons blended with seductive stares across my table at one another I felt his other hand reach beneath my desk and come to rest upon my knee. My breath caught in my throat, and I reached down with my hand to place it upon his own.

"Alexis might get scared at this." I said to him. He started to pull his hand back, but I held it in place saying "but Lexi isn't. Your date with Lexi is going well enough that she enjoys having your touch."

"Good to know." Jeremiah replied quietly. My heart skipped a beat as his warm, powerful thumb brushed over my shaved knee just a bit below the hem of my skirt.

"It's nice to know my legs are appreciated." I replied releasing my hold of his hand and pretending to lick the back of the pen spoon.

I looked up at him and asked, "shall we dance?"

Jeremiah let go of my knee and said, "I definitely need practice with that too."

We worked carefully and quickly. He shoved my desk back to where it was and pulled up a romantic song playlist on his phone while I picked up some clothing and junk from my floor to clear a dance floor. As I was bent over, I felt his warm hand caress my buttocks and I glanced over at him realizing that he was touching me worshipfully with a distant stare in his eyes. He shook his head and let go of me as soft, low R&B music thumped lightly in the background. My mind wanted him to continue. I don't know how, but I wanted him to hike my skirt up and claim my body as his own for his pleasure. I swallowed down these desires as I hastily tossed what was in my hands over into my laundry hamper before turning back around to him.

"Sorry, I uhh…" He stammered.

"Shhh…" I replied.

"You're not going to offend or anger Lexi. That's why you're practicing with her. So, you can be ready for Alexis. Okay?"

"Thank you so much." Jeremiah replied.

I smiled at him as I straightened out my clothing a bit and said, "do you know how to dance?"

He shook his head, and I took his hands guiding them to my hips. I felt sad that they weren't more supple for his pleasure, but they were what I had to work with. I then wrapped my hands up over his shoulders around the back of his neck staring up at him sensually as we slowly began to sway back and forth to the beat of the music.

"That's it?" He asked.

"For a slow dance, yes." I replied.

"The real pleasure of the dance, isn't the motion, though." I continued as I leaned in sensually close to him. I could smell his manly musk and as I drew near, I felt his firm bulge press against my body. He winced but I just danced in a little closer to him saying "it's those times the principle is busy annoying other people, and you get to touch."

We swayed back and forth as I felt his bulge stiffen with erection. The soothing, romantic music filled our ears and soon I came to rest my head against his broad shoulders. His hands quit their post at my hips and began to work their way down across my buttocks caressing and claiming my flesh as they went bringing sighs from my mouth. I turned my head up to him and any illusion of being two boys screwing around fled from between us.

He knelt his head down and I puckered feeling his warm, powerful lips caress my own as we kissed sweetly.

He raised his head, and one last withering look of fear crossed his eyes before I let go of his shoulder with my right hand and ran it sensually down across his chest. I slid it down between us finding its way to his crotch where I wrapped my small fingers around his massive manhood feeling the powerful member bulge in my hands. I wordlessly smiled and he knelt in to kiss me again. Some small part of my intellect screamed in the back of my head that this was my buddy, and we weren't gay, but I hushed it because Lexi was about to get fucking laid and I was definitely going to go along for that ride. Besides, look at how happy I'm making Jeremiah. I never thought I would be able to bring this much joy to my best friend ever.

"The dance was a success. You brought me home and discovered that my parents are out for the weekend. I invited you up to my room…" I narrated to him.

"Now… what are you going to do to me?" I whispered to him breathily as I began to gently massage his cock. He let go of my hips and gently slid me back towards my bed. He stripped off his shorts letting his powerfully erect member fly free, and my eyes went wide as I reviewed how much bigger it was than my own. I had only ever seen it in passing during locker room time while he was relaxed before, so I never knew the full potential of its size. I wrapped my fingers around it and gave him pleading eyes. He cocked his head to the side and leaned in and we shared another deep and passionate kiss. This time, I felt his tongue enter my mouth and I moaned at the sensation as I felt his cock grow hot and firm in my hand. His hands busied themselves with lifting the hem of my blouse and I let go of his cock and raised my arms so that he could strip it off from me leaving me there in my sister's skirt and red bra.

"You're beautiful." He whispered as he leaned back to behold me in my sister's bra. I did a little shimmy and giggled as he proceeded to peel my sister's tight skirt off my body leaving me there in a bra and panties. I felt a hint of disappointment that I couldn't fill out that bra with a beautiful rack of breasts for him to play with and that my panties sported a little bulge of my own, albeit many times smaller than his. I looked up into his eyes as he trailed his gaze deliriously along my body gasping with desire. My heart exploded with love for him in that moment as I realized that he accepted me, small breasts, pathetic thighs, and cock of my own. I wished desperately that I had large breasts for him to play with and a wet, tight pussy for him to fuck, but such was not the case. Despite this, he still wanted me sexually. We kissed once more and, this time, I grabbed his shirt pulling it up over his head as we awkwardly danced around our own arms. I ran my hands across the beautifully sculpted muscles of his arms and chest drinking in the masculine sensuality of his body feeling suddenly freed of any inhibitions. I relished the thought of relinquishing my identity as the dweeby boy Jordan, wearing his sister's underwear and fucking around with his buddy on a Saturday afternoon. In that moment, I embraced my identity as Lexi, a girl about to get laid by the Varsity team's basketball center.

I wrapped my fingers around his cock once more and this is all the invitation he needed as he gently pressed me back making me sit onto his bed. I now stared at his cock before me, so close I could just…

I blew out a sigh.

"What are you doing?" Jeremiah whispered down to me as I stared at his cock.

"Working up my courage." I replied.

"For what?"

I swallowed down my inhibitions and opened my mouth leaning forward to welcome his ripe, firm cock into me. I didn't know what to expect, but felt pleasantly surprised that his cock didn't have any particularly bad taste. Rather, it tasted like normal flesh, just the same as if I had licked my forearm or something. It did have a slight, saltiness at the tip that was actually pleasant as long as I ignored all the ponderous implications that it represented. More than taste, his cock had an incredible textural experience. It seemed to 'fit' naturally into my mouth although I could never venture to fit all of it in. His shaft throbbed lightly letting me feel the quickened pulse of his heartbeat as his smooth tip lushly filled my mouth.

The effect of my act on Jeremiah seemed to be the most powerful experience of all as he shuddered and began panting chanting "Oh, my god, Oh, my god… Jordan."

I let go just long enough to reply, "call me Lexi."

And then I returned to my feast of his beautiful man flesh watching his knees buckle when I wiggled my tongue along the bottom of his frenulum. I don't know why girls complain about this. This is awesome as hell. It's like a fucking remote control for a boy's body and the feeling of incredible power that I had over him in that moment filled me with glee the likes of which I had never imagined possible.

"That…feels… incredible…" Jeremiah gasped as his legs weakened such that he was about to stumble over.

"I can't… I just can't…" He began as his whole body shifted towards me pressing his cock in deeper towards me. I retracted my head feeling a strange sense of disappointment and yet, at the same time, salvation. I felt ashamed of how weak I had been, clearly probably border-line gay and now I had outed myself to my best friend but also… well… to myself I suppose. I started rehearsing my speech about how I was just playing the role and apologizing for going too far with it but then Jeremiah finished saying

"I can't resist."

He shoved me back and I sprawled across his bed. Before I could even react, he had mounted me, and I looked lovingly up across the mountain of muscle rising over my chest. His warm, fuzzy balls rested on my chest right between the cups of my sister's bra as I felt his warm, powerful legs wrapping around either side of me.

He looked down at me with a bizarre, glazed over stare in his eye like whatever intellect drove him had given way to mad desire. He mustered the last of his will to whisper, "please don't stop… Lexi."

I smiled and took his cock into my mouth once more resting my elbows on his knees and wrapping my hand around the base of his cock where I could not quite reach with my lips. I knew that he would probably like his balls cupped and massaged while we did this too. I regretted that I didn't have a pair of awesome, gorgeous breasts to warmly snuggle his balls against while he reaped sexual pleasure from my body, but I biologically could provide no such thing. I had no choice but to settle for reaching beneath with my left hand and holding his balls as best as I could with my fingertips. This wasn't easy though as the position was awkward and it became even more difficult as he began thrusting into my mouth. Terror filled me that I might accidentally bite him, and I feared the repercussions of this as I stretched my mouth as wide as I possibly could. His throbbing, full hot cock felt like it was going to explode in my mouth as he madly began shoving while his hips pulsated in rapid rhythm. I realized what they meant by 'face-fucking' as any illusion of active seduction on my part disappeared within his thrusts such that all I did was hold my mouth open and he sought out the pleasure it could provide.

I pondered how, for a girl, this would probably be terrifying. She would have no background, no experience, no preparation for something like this. I smirked considering how that stuck up pussy Alexis sure as hell couldn't do this, she would be all screaming and crying and pleading for him to stop before he even mounted her.

Luckily, I'm not really a girl.

Although a virgin, I knew a bit of what Jeremiah was experiencing. I knew the pace I took with my right hand on those lonely cold nights with nothing but lewd pictures on the internet for company. He now took that pace within my mouth and no fear filled me as I carefully breathed through my nose during his retraction pulses so I could hold my breath when he would thrust once again deep in my mouth driving the head of his cock dangerously close to my throat. I figured this must be like my hand, but maybe a hundred times better and pride swelled within my heart at the thought that I could produce such overwhelming pleasure for my best friend. This pride cut short slightly as the taste of saltiness started saturating my mouth again and I realized that I didn't have a plan for how to handle the inevitable aftermath of this.

It was only a matter of time before he started squirting…

I pondered spitting it out or something like that or pulling him away when he started cumming, but I knew this would be tantamount to blue-balling. Besides, an orgasm is better when you continue to stroke through the orgasm itself rather than just starting it and leaving your cock laying there squirting cum all over the place while you don't touch it. Alexis may be too much of a pussy to swallow cum, but I knew that I wasn't, and I knew that Jeremiah's experience would be ten times better if I "girl-ed" up and let him finish cumming in my mouth. With this in mind, I bravely welcomed his cock in even as he began squirting hot, sticky masses of cum deep into my throat almost choking me. He stopped thrusting and I only slightly undulated my tongue against the bottom of his cock knowing the razor-thin difference between the paradise of an orgasm and the painful tickle of too much sexual pleasure. Knowing he would absolutely love it, I took advantage of his static nature to reach under again and wrap my fingers around his balls, now drawn up tight and firm against his pulsating body. I cupped them with my hand and massaged them gently helping ever last bit of cum he had come out from them so I could drink it down for him.

He moaned and I looked up at him feeling a bit better seeing all my valiant effort was worth it as his face contorted into unimaginable pleasure and his body shivered as he gasped and panted while his cock continued to fill my mouth full of cum. I needed to swallow, but it was difficult with his cock in my mouth so once I could take it no more, I broke my hold of his cock swallowing down his sticky cum and gasping for breath.

He flopped off from me as a look of horror crossed his face. "Oh, god, Jordan, I'm so sorry. I'm so sorry. I didn't mean to…" He spluttered and trembled as he lay there in bed next to me with his still slickly damp cock pulsing lightly drizzling out the last few drops of cum. I sat up and turned towards him. I wiggled my jaw slightly feeling the tension in the muscles.

"Oh, shit, I didn't mean to hurt you. I'm so sorry…" Jeremiah sputtered, but I cut him off by leaning over to him and lightly kissing the tip of his cock before licking away the last drizzle of his cum. He groaned appreciatively then looked down at me and blinked in surprise.

"I'm not hurt. We're okay." I said.

He nodded with his eyes still wide and terrified. I turned to face him as I sat on the bed and placed a hand on his chest. I smiled and asked, "did that feel good?"

"Incredible beyond my wildest imagination. I'm sorry I… took it to far and…."

"Nothing to be sorry for." I said quietly.

He looked at me somberly.

I smiled supportively and said, "I'm *glad* that I could give my best friend such incredible pleasure. I uhh…" I chuckled and continued, "I didn't exactly have a plan in place for this and I didn't know if I would be able to do that. I'm surprised to hear it felt good. I was afraid I would mess it up somehow."

"That's what you were afraid of?" He asked.

I rolled my eyes lightly and continued, "that and if I would bite you on accident."

"You're not worried that this might mean were gay now?" He said with a cringe.

I looked down across myself. With the taste of another boys cum in my mouth and my cock tucked beneath the central panel of a girl's panties the word 'gay' seemed both appropriate and inappropriate at the same time.

"Let's not get ahead of ourselves. I was just helping you practice for when you do get a girl to suck you."

Jeremiah swallowed hard and said, "that was one hell of a practice. I feel horrible for shoving you down like that. I wish I could make it up to you."

I pouted lightly reviewing his cock noticing a red-ringed 'highwater mark' that I had managed to smear onto it with my sister's lipstick. I smiled lightly at how impressively far down the meaty shaft it lay. I had to admit that I was better at being a girl than I had ever been at being a boy. I closed my eyes and asked myself what I wanted. Honestly, after all that thrusting and mad-desire driven violence, I needed a reprieve, but I also didn't want to be alone. I feared that, if I fled now, this would only be some icky, terrible thing we did once and regretted for the rest of our lives. I shivered lightly as I felt the bizarre desire for Jeremiah to wrap me up in a warm hug and tell me that he loved me.

"Hold me while I lay on your chest." I said. It was the closest thing I could conjure up to the truth in that moment as to what I wanted from him.

"What? That's even more…" he began to protest.

"Just trust that it's what I want in this moment. Okay? Lay back and spread out your arm so I can put my head on your chest." I replied softly, but firmly.

To my shock, the larger stronger boy succumbed to my demand. He lay flat on his back while I cuddled up with my shoulder under his armpit. I felt his arm wrap around my back and pull me in close to him.

I sighed as the side of my head rested on his warm, powerful chest. I delicately placed my hand across his chest. A rhythmic throbbing filled my left ear and I recognized it as his heartbeat pounding sure and strong deep within his chest, I gently wrapped my leg over his own feeling a bit self-conscious about the fact that, through the whole affair, I still had my sister's strappy sandals on my feet. I smiled thinking about how I would make the perfect porn-star girl, wearing my red lingerie and high-heels. I snuggled in tight to him with this happy thought fluttering through my brain.

"Is… this… helping?" He asked, slowly.

"Yes… Aftercare is…reassuring." I replied quietly.

We lay there for a few minutes just breathing together. I listened as his heartbeat began to slow down as the panic from what we had just done left his mind.

Without thinking about it, my hand began slowly descending along his muscular abdomen. I wasn't even conscious of what I was doing until I felt the firm tip of his cock brush along under my fingers. He groaned appreciatively as my fingers instinctively wrapped around his shaft feeling it grow ripe at my touch.

"What are you doing?" Jeremiah asked.

I must admit, I didn't really have a plan for this. I heard his heartbeat quicken once more.

"It's so much bigger than mine." I murmured appreciatively. His cock was still slightly wet from my saliva, but its warmth still felt reassuring to my touch.

"No way." He snorted.

"I'm not competing, I'm just… admiring." I whispered as I stared at the tip of his cock. I felt his fingers press lightly against my side and then slide down along my hips finding the lacey hem of my sister's panties. Jeremiah began tugging them off from me.

"What are you doing?" I asked. Even as I asked this, I submissively raised my hips to help him in stripping off my panties. Same as if I had been a real girl quietly helping him gain access to my sweet, hungry pussy. He leaned up letting me slide off his arm and lay on the bed as he kneeled in front of me pulling off my panties. I cringed lightly as my sad little cock and two unwanted balls fell out from the panel which had hid them as nothing more than a small bulge up until this point in time. My cringe turned to a gasp as I felt my tiny little penis slide over the top of his massive burly cock which held it aloft. I shuddered lightly and smiled as I saw his huge cock propping up my own and I enjoyed the warmth and the feeling of his powerful pulse trembling along the bottom of my cock.

"You really are much smaller than me." He said in a flat, matter of fact matter.
I looked down at our overlapping cocks. It was truly no comparison. I looked back up and saw him staring at me warmly.

"Do you wish it was bigger?" He asked.

I bit my lower lip for a moment before replying with the full weight of honesty burdening my words "I wish it was a vagina."

He blinked at me in surprise. I sighed and confessed "I wish I could be a girl for you. I wish I was a real girl. We would play video games and basketball and all the same stuff we always do and then you would pull me in close and tell me you love me and take me out and stuff but…" I grimaced as I shook my head saying "Sorry, just… stupid. Forget I said anythi-"

"Shhh…" Jeremiah cut me off with his warm, deep voice.

I looked up at him. We had passed through any illusions of 'practice' or 'play' by this point, as I had just laid my heart out on the line like an idiot. He ran warm hands lovingly along my shoulders and down across the sides of my chest and lightly up the sides of my legs before returning them to my shoulders. He gently caressed the side of my cheek and his touch felt tender and warm.

"I had no idea you were so beautiful." He said quietly.

I smiled sweetly at his compliment.

"Girls are always so bitchy and mean. They stare at you angrily when you try to talk to them. They grumble about you to their friends behind your back. Other than pussy, there's not a whole lot that's pleasant about girls. I always wished I could have a girlfriend who was like you. You know, a girl like my best friend who was chill and nice." He said.

As he spoke, he continued running his hands appreciatively across my body making me grateful that I had shaved for him. "You just gave me the most incredible pleasure I had ever experienced in my entire life." He reached down and wrapped a large warm hand over my cock and balls making me sharply inhale and rise my body to his touch. He continued "Since you're not a girl, you won't be making me regret it for weeks on end with your complaining about me not appreciating the time you gave me a blowjob more. You're a boy. You know what boys want and you know how to make it happen."

I nodded silently even as I arched my head back and closed my eyes feeling his thumb begin caressing the side of my little cock head.

"God, your body is so gorgeous, clean, pretty, and tight. I don't think I can resist you much longer." Jeremiah mused as one hand still massaged my cock while his other ran along my thigh sliding occasionally around to caress my buttocks.

"Then don't resist. Do what you want with my body." I said breathily.

I felt his cock drop low sliding across my balls and down between my legs. I regretted not having a proper vagina for him to smash, but I could tell where he was going with this, and I wasn't going to deny it to him even if I was a bit nervous not knowing what to expect. I thrust my hips forward a bit and reached down beneath me grabbing my own butt cheeks and pulling them apart. I bit my lower lip fearful of what might happen next but telling myself that Jeremiah wouldn't hurt me. His thumbs soon joined my fingers as he spread me open, and I felt his hot cock pressing in towards me. A small, dull pain filled my buttocks mixed with incredible sensation of warmth and power pressing deep into me. He thrust and I gasped as his cock caught slightly on my flesh spreading my sphincter apart.

"You, okay?" Jeremiah asked.

I nodded and replied, "just give me a few seconds to loosen up for you." He brought his arms up and rested on his elbows leaning on either side of my head as he held his position filling me with his warmth and power deep inside my buttocks but not pressing in any deeper than he already was.

"Can I kiss you?" he asked.

"Yes." I replied sweetly with a girlish smile as he leaned in, and we shared a passionate kiss. The kiss felt like paradise as I hung longingly onto his lips drinking in the masculine power of his essence. My body relaxed and adopted its role of impromptu 'girl' letting him penetrate deliciously deeper inside of me. My intestines ached and my body protested, but beyond this was a strange sense of forbidden pleasure which I couldn't quite put my mind onto. I decided to focus on the sensation of him, being so close, so powerful, so in control and so I stared longingly up into his eyes as he gasped and blinked in surprise.

"Good?" I asked.

"You feel incredible."

"Wonderful. Find your pleasure."

He smiled and said "I will. But first…" He reached a hand down and found my cock with it. He slowly began to thrust as he massaged my cock bringing moans of pleasure to my mouth. "If you were a girl, you would get to feel pleasure. It's only fair I give you an orgasm as well."

He began thrusting slowly as he pumped his hand wrapped around my cock and the entire lower half of my body was under his control. I could do nothing other than let go of my now well-spread butt cheeks and reach up to wrap my hands around his powerful shoulders. I could conjure no protest for what he was doing to me even though it involved pleasuring my own cock, which I hated. He pumped his hand bringing undulating pleasure along my cock while he thrust deep inside me teaching my body how to experience new definitions of pleasure deep inside. I leaned up as hard as I could and kissed him passionately as I felt my body explode with delicious sensations. I tried to hold the kiss as long as I could, but I couldn't manage it more than a few seconds before I succumbed to the incredible orgasm boiling throughout my veins as both hand and cock pressed my squirting to ever higher limits and taught me joys that I didn't know existed. I tipped my head back and silently screamed into the air, forcing my mouth to remain quiet lest my parents hear us downstairs. He continued thrusting rhythmically and my pleasure over boiled into some disgusting tickling sensation inside of me as my body continued orgasming even after all my cum had been depleted. That new pleasure Jeremiah had taught me took hold and replaced the tickling as the pressure from his powerful cock grew intense deep inside my body and his thrusting became urgent. I lolled my head down slowly in my sex drunken state just in time to see him shove deep inside me so hard that my nuts rested on his stomach, and he grunted in orgasm. He began to retract suddenly but I did the only thing I could do and wrapped my legs around behind him grabbing onto his firm buttock with my ankles, still strapped into my sister's black leather heels. I cupped his buttocks with my heeled feet and flexed my thighs pulling him ever deeper inside of my body where he could enjoy his orgasm properly enveloped in the inviting warmth and tender caress of my flesh. I smiled up at him as I felt his cock stiffen as he shivered and groaned.

"Go ahead and cum inside me. I want you to." I whispered reassuringly to him as tremors of pleasure rippled through his powerful body and his cock squirt hot cum deep inside my ass. I wiggled my body sensually bringing forth fresh gasps from his mouth and reorganizing my position so as to get better purchase with my feet wrapped around his backside. He collapsed across me and I breathed a deep sigh of relief and held him tight resting my small head on his powerful shoulder drinking in his musky scent for a while before I could sense his sexual energy waning. I released him from my cross-legged gasp. After a few moments, he retracted. I grimaced and whimpered as the cock which had been inside me suddenly slipped out. He collapsed in exhaustion onto the bed next to me. I rolled over and wrapped a hand around his shoulder and cuddled close to my best friend.

"Jordan." He said.

"Yes?" I asked.

"Would you go to the spring formal with me?" He asked.

No practice.

No girl.

No fucking around.

He was legit asking me out.

I lay there in shock for a moment before replying, "Absolutely."

"Really?" He said seeming to perk up a bit.

I kissed him sweetly before continuing, "Yes. Besides, I have the perfect dress for the occasion."

"What is it?" He asked.

I licked my lips and smiled coyly before replying, "it will be a surprise, something I'm looking forward to you seeing me in."

I snuggled in close to him laying piled in a tumble of arms, legs, torsos, and love before I continued, "same as the lingerie I have in mind for afterwards."

Castrated By My Crush

My fingers slipped and I nearly dropped the vanilla-scented candle down alongside my other instruments of worship on the desk. The odd assortment boasted KY jelly, a steel ruler, a pair of treasured, pink elastic hairbands (mailed to me by goddess), a set of syringe needles and other exquisite instruments of torture.

I arranged my laptop on the cheap box-store desk next to my bed, making sure that it had plenty of charge in the battery as my acts of worship could take me anywhere in the house. Similar to Pavlov's dog, the very act of preparing for worship made my cock grow hard and my pulse feel weak.

I suppose out there, in the normal world, a guy like me would look forward to Friday night as a chance to go drinking with friends at a bar somewhere. Perhaps he would flirt with some girl in hopes of taking her home but, I'm not that guy. For me, Friday night is not a time of loud music and crowded bars. It's a sacred time set aside for the acts of worship which bring healing to my soul while the rest of the weekend is set aside as a time of healing for my body from those same acts of worship. My trembling hands opened my laptop and connected it to the private server from which my goddess speaks.

An eternity passed as I sat at the desk staring at the loading screen. Terrified thoughts filled my head as I contemplated if I had not submitted enough tribute to her or perhaps if I had angered my goddess in some other way. To my relief, the screen flashed to life, and I saw my goddess, looking just as ethereal and beautiful as the day I first saw her, sitting calmly alighted upon her overstuffed couch of a throne.

Jenna smiled as she saw me, and I gasped with my eyes wide in delight and terror as my body instinctively prepared itself for both pleasure and pain. Every detail of her body seemed as if it had been carved by a Renaissance sculptor. Her bobbed blonde hair danced lightly against the edge of her pristine jawline right where her high, dainty cheeks touched against her elegant, slender neck. Her cute, upturned pert little nose crinkled lightly as piercing blue eyes gained a slight, malevolent twinkle. Her eyes bore the same kind of playful twinkle a cat gets when it spies a lone mouse out and ready for the pouncing. She leaned back against one side of the chair on her elbows and her petite yet powerfully compact body seemed to glisten, even without the goofy filters girls use sometimes to improve their appearance on social. She wore a low-cut pink blouse, through which her warm, smooth breasts pressed outward against the criminally thin fabric as her perky little nipples poked through testifying to a lack of bra beneath it. She sat sideways on the throne with her delicious, smooth legs slung casually over the arm of the white couch letting her beautiful little bare feet dangle and dance over the edge as her gorgeous, ripe buttocks rested upon the cushion of the throne encased in nothing more than a pair of spandex shorts that barely covered her. Her sensual butt cheeks poked out sweetly from beneath the black edged hem hinted at exquisitely sexual organs just beyond the world of my sight. My eyes glazed over as they trailed along the sensual treasure that was her glory. It felt like staring into the gilded vault of Fort Knox or perhaps directly at the sun as simultaneous memories of beauty and pain crashed through my mind.

“Good evening, Jordan.” She said calmly, but firmly. “Good evening, Mistress Jenna.” I replied, bowing my head low to her. “I was afraid you had not received my tribute.”

“Your earlier sacrifices of money have been received.” She said with an impish smile before shifting her body to face towards me and leaning in close to the computer before continuing “like a good little boy, you proved you know how to follow orders. However, you, of all people, should know that our relationship has moved past those little trifles. I haven’t made you suffer financially for months now. It’s so much more fulfilling to make you suffer directly. Are the burn wounds from our last worship session healed?”

“I think so, Mistress Jenna.” I replied.

A sly smile spread across her parted lips as she said “good. I feared this week may be ruined by what we did last week. God, that was so exciting. Making you jerk all the way up to near orgasm before forcing you to fuck the flame of a lit candle. You do know that your pathetic screams are the only part of you that makes my pussy wet. I could almost smell the cooking flesh of your delicate little frenulum from here." Her voice dropped as she said this. Her breathing grew hoarse and shallow with desire. Her hand dropped to her crotch, and she began rubbing it slightly saying "I screamed too, by the way, later that night. As Jason pinned me under his six-foot-five inch, two-hundred and fifty-pound body to the bed and split my delicate little pussy lips wide open to shove his thick, ten-inch cock deep inside my womanhood. I couldn't do anything but submit my body to his power. It felt like getting fucked by a hurricane." She panted and her body shivered as she continued, "despite all that, the only thing I could think of was your worthless, sick, little cock cooking over that open flame. Seeing your face contorted in pain and hearing you scream and beg me to let you stop. I fantasized, Jordan, I fantasized about burning your cock all the way off. That fantasy made me squirt my sweet little womanly juices all over my husband's giant fucking tool as he skewered me alive with it. It was only then that I felt him squirt his hot, powerful sperm all over my soft little insides."

Jenna shivered and trembled as her eyes grew distant and she sat silent for a moment. I squinted as her face fell. Her voice changed and her expression softened as she continued in a tone which trembled between sadness and banality as she muttered almost to herself "why the fuck am I only able to cum when I think about hurting you?" She bowed her head and whispered to herself, "what's wrong with me?"

"Huh?" I asked.

Jenna looked back up into the camera and said, "Jordan, can we talk?"

"Talk? We're talking now?"

"No, no… not dominate, just… talk?"

"I'm listening."

She sighed and her eyes turned dreamy and distant as she asked "do you remember the first time I hurt you?"

"I'll never forget it as long as I live." I replied as the memory came crashing back to me.

"God, it was so magical. April our Junior year, you asked me to go to prom with you, and when I said 'no' you leaned in for a kiss." Jenna said with a light giggle.

"You did an excellent job of teaching me that my proper place is beneath you, Mistress." I replied.

"I remember the warm feeling of your shoulders in my hands. I remember thinking, 'am I actually going to do this?' before I drove my knee up between your legs. It seemed so light a blow to me. I didn't really have the room to swing my whole leg and kick you properly. It felt like the kind of desperate, flailing kick a teenage girl would give. But, my god, I felt them. I felt your nuts and erect cock squish against my kneecap. Then I saw your face. Your eyes nearly bugged out of your skull as you dropped to your knees. I remember that moment of revelation…I…" She gasped, enthralled with the power of the memory. She placed her left hand against the center of her chest saying "I… did that. I did that to a boy. I literally destroyed your existence and forced you to experience hell on earth for a while. I had never done anything like that before. I didn't really think I could even do anything like that. I never knew I had such power. It felt so intoxicating, and, at the same time, terror filled my mind. I remember fear stalking my every step as I ran away from you while you lay writhing on the ground that day. I stayed up all night imagining you finding some teacher, telling her what I had done to you. I could almost feel myself getting expelled for fighting."

She trembled slightly as she continued "but… you didn't. You kept your silence and a part of me felt gratitude for that, even as I avoided you for the rest of school. I could feel your hungry eyes on me in every class but every time I turned to look at you, you would cower like a beaten dog." A sinister smile spread across Jenna's face as she continued "God, I loved that. I loved seeing you so weak and pathetic and knowing that I did that to you. My whole life I always felt like I wasn't important but, with a single kick, I put you in hell and gave you such horrible trauma that you never dared raise your head in my presence again." Jenna swallowed hard and continued, "hurting you unlocked something incredible inside of me. Something I didn't even know existed. I wanted to hurt men. I fantasized about hurting you again. I would rub my little clit at night as I dreamed about holding your feet up and driving my heel into your balls listening to your anguished screams. I dared not tell anyone about it. That's why I married the most powerful man that I could find. I dared not trust myself in the same room with any man who couldn't bench-press me."

"I'm… the reason you… ended up with Jason?" I asked slowly in confusion.

Jenna giggled "'ended up with?' Oh, sad little boy, you of all people know I have the power to make any man do anything I want him to do. You're all just cute little tinker-toys I can wind up and play with however I like, and you all still love me for it no matter how much pain I put you in. No, 'ending up with' was never part of the equation. I simply picked Jason out and married him. He never had a choice in the matter."

Jenna leaned in and whispered intimately, "In a way, though, yes, you did contribute to my marriage. I suppose hurting you taught me what I was looking for in a husband. Just think, Jordan, if you had actually been with me, let's say… my husband…"

She lowered her voice and her face softened as she licked her lips before saying sensually "I would have killed you by now, Jordan." A smile spread across her lips as she continued "I would have killed you slowly, and I would have enjoyed every second of it. I would have tortured you until your sad little heart stopped beating. Then I would have desecrated your corpse by grinding my cunt on top of your lifeless body until I cummed all over it. God, imagine the DNA evidence for the district attorney on that one. I would… I would… I would have been executed or living in prison by now." Jenna's eyes went wide, and she trembled in a manner quite unbecoming of a goddess as she continued, "that's why I married Jason. He's so strong and powerful, I can't do anything but submit in his presence. It's for his own safety, too. Ever since you opened my eyes, hurting men has been an addiction of mine and I couldn't find any release for that dark, primal, sadistic urge."

Jenna gestured towards the screen saying, "That is, until the magic of the internet came into my life. I offered my services. Most simps and subs weren't serious about it. They cum when I tell them they can't, they don't follow directions, scoff at my tributes." Jenna scrunched up her nose and snorted, saying "pathetic wannabes. But then, lo and behold, the boy who started it all, came crawling back to me, craving, of all things, more abuse."

Jenna leaned in close to the screen and said, "I never told you this before, but my heart felt so happy to see you again when you subscribed to me. Hurting you again after all those years felt like a dream come true."

"Why are you talking this way?" I asked.

She blinked in surprise and sat back on the couch crossing her arms uncomfortably. She bowed her head slightly and said, "I just wanted to talk a bit, for real that is, before we get started with torturing you. You see, tonight is a special night. For both of us."

"Why?"

A small smile spread across her face as she said "I'll show you a big surprise. Close your eyes."

I did as instructed. In the darkness, I heard a shuffling sound followed by my goddess's voice as she continued.

"Okay, Jordan, open your eyes."

Jenna's face filled the camera as she crouched in front of it. She held in front of her a tapered white, plastic stick. It bore the superficially unremarkable, but contextually critical, two pink lines. My mouth fell open as Jenna smiled softly at me saying "remember how I said I could feel Jason's squirting sperm all over my insides?"

"Yeah."

"Well, one landed right on top of my sweet little egg."

I trembled, not sure which emotion I should have been feeling at that moment. Excitement for Jenna, jealousy of Jason, fear for my own future…?

"I'm going to be a mother, Jordan." Jenna said. Not a single hint of sexuality, domination, sadism, or power-play, lay in her voice. She spoke simply as a woman relating an exciting life transition to a close friend.

"Co…congratulations…" I stammered back.

She set the stick down and slid back from the screen a bit saying "thank you, Jordan. Like I said, tonight's a special night." She sighed and said with a determined voice, "this will be our last night together."

"What!?" I gasped back in shock and horror.

"Jordan… I'm pregnant." She said with a contortion of pain on her face. The facade of my goddess crumbled lightly under that look. "I'm going to be a mother."

For the first time in my life, fear crossed the face of my goddess.

"A mother… me… mothering… a baby." She began to pant in terror as she shook her head.
She gestured at the screen saying, "do you think I'm going to be torturing simps while I'm…what? breastfeeding my infant? Teaching my child how to walk? Joining the PTA or some bullshit?" She raised both her hands saying, "We're converting this room into a nursery, Jordan."

"No, no, no… you can't."

"Can't?" She said back with a sinister growl.

"Sorry, Goddess, I spoke out of turn."

Visible emotion crossed her face as she said "it's time I grew up, Jordan. It's time we grew up, Jordan." She shivered lightly as she continued "it's time to let go."

I shuddered and tears began to stream down my face.

She swallowed hard and continued, "that's why tonight is going to be very special."

I wiped my ears away as she continued, "You were my first, Jordan. You were the one who made me fall in love with torturing men. The other subs, the wannabes and horn-dogs, I just closed their accounts. I told them I quit without saying why. I even reimbursed the last tribute checks that I've received this week. I didn't tell them why. They don't deserve to know. None of them ever formed anything real with me, just treated me like some pay-for-pain hooker. You, however…"

She shuddered and whispered "Jordan, I haven't even told my parents about the child yet. You are literally the first person outside of my husband to know that I'm pregnant."

She stared intimately into the screen at me and continued, "that's how much I love you."

My jaw dropped open.

"You… love me?"

She smiled saying, "in the sadistic way that I love feasting on your experience of pain."

She raised a finger and said, "I'm not simply closing your account like

I did the others. For you, I'm going to do something very special. I'm going to finally go all the way with a man. I'm going to indulge in my final, darkest fantasy. This is the last torture session that I'm going to conduct. You were my first, and you will be my last. After tonight, I will never do this again."

"But…"

She leaned in close and said, "sometimes growth requires sacrifice. We're going to hold each other's hands and sever this part of our lives cleanly away."

"What do you mean?"

"Do you remember that box I sent you? Several months ago? The one I told you to never open."

"Yes"

"Go get it."

I quickly left, dashing through my apartment to the closet. I cursed my clothing as I flung it about desperately searching for that box. At long last, I dug it out and blew the dust off the top of the cardboard. The box was about two feet long and very heavy. My name and address were neatly written on top in scripted, effeminate handwriting while a massive amount over-paid postage stamps decorated an entire side.

I returned to my bedroom with the box. Jenna smiled as she saw it saying "good boy. You know how to follow instructions. Did it drive you mad not knowing what was inside all these months? Please say that it did. I like imagining you lying awake at night whimpering in frustration wondering what lay inside the forbidden box that I had sent you."

"I did feel, curious, but I knew that when the time came you would instruct me as to what to do with it."

Jenna's face fell and she cocked her head to the side lightly. "You trust me the way a rabbit trusts the wolf with his teeth around its neck… that is so fucking pathetic that it's hot. Open the box, little boy, and keep looking up at the camera. You're not allowed to ask questions until you have unpacked the entire thing. I want to see your expression as what the surprise I have in store for you reveals itself."

My hands trembled as I pried open the packaging. Digging through I found a Ziplock bag with extremely reinforced looking, tight, rubber bands, a shiny, metallic tool that looked to be a pair of pliers, but with metal protrusions jutting out from the side. I pursed my lips and looked back up at her.

"Keep looking, it gets more exciting as you go." She said as she seemed to peek over the edge of the laptop screen like she was trying to look down in the box. Next, I dug out a pair of metal rails, a set of inter-locked metal plates with a stand and bearing a two-inch diameter hole in between them, A crossbar fitted with a locking latch, a few stand pieces, some odd-looking electronic components, and a heavy, sharp, triangular shaped blade.

My breath shuddered in my chest as my hands trembled while I ran them along the blade. We had played with torture of my cock and balls for sure but this… this looked serious. This blade wasn't designed to hurt, it was designed…

…to sever.

I swallowed hard and looked back up at the screen to see Jenna staring back at me, her eyes wide in delight. She asked, "does it excite you knowing the blade in your hands will soon be biting through your flesh?"

I shuddered lightly.

She crinkled her nose and said, "I thought you were serious about our relationship."

"I am, I am… I just…" I set the blade down carefully on the table.

"It's a guillotine, isn't it?" I said.

Jenna shrugged saying "A guillotine is designed to cut off a man's head and end his life. The custom-built little device in front of you is designed to cut off a man's other head and end his life as a man. They are very different things."

"I never knew you hated me this much." I muttered in shock.

"Hate!?" Jenna shrieked. She leaned in close to the screen and said "Jordan! How dare you accuse me of hating you."

I squinted at her in confusion.

She continued speaking passionately, "I love you more than my husband. I've loved you ever since you opened my eyes to how delicious it feels to hurt a man. That device in front of you cost over five-hundred dollars. It is a testament to how deeply I love you. Not my husband, not the other subs, no one else, Jordan, nobody…"

She panted as her eyes went wide and she continued "is going to experience castration at my hands other than you."

"You would take my sex away from me?" I asked in fear.

"As long as you are a man, you will be under my spell, fully in my control. If I hide, you will find me. If I run, you will follow. Your life, your destiny is to be destroyed by me." Jenna's eyes glistened as she spoke.

"You know this is true." Jenna continued, firmly.

I bowed my head.

"I considered sending you a gun." She said quietly.

I looked up into her eyes intimately. I would say that love passed between us, but our relationship could not be defined in such a limiting concept. No word, no image, no metaphor, no logic, nothing in this world above it or below it can explain the beautiful brutality of my worship of this great goddess.

“I would to kill you, but I want to kill you as a man, not as a person. So, I will sever the man from the person. What’s left of you may live on as a non-gendered person from this day forward. You already have a good name for it. Jordan, could be male, female, or nothing at all.”

I smiled at her lightly. I looked off distantly for a moment thinking about my future. A future free from desire, lust, control… and pleasure.

They would all leave me in the same, fell swoop of a blade.

I nodded quietly.

She smiled lightly saying “Good boy. I’m looking forward to staring into your soft brown eyes and seeing the light of manhood die within them as the pathetic excuse for a cock and balls falls free from your body.” As she said this, she leaned back and slid a hand down her spandex shorts to begin fingering herself.

“Command me, goddess.”

“Ohh…” Jenna said as she shivered in pleasure saying “you always do know how to please me, Jordan. In your own deliciously wretched little way. I’m going to enjoy killing your manhood tonight but, first, I want to see you strip for me like a good boy. Show me that sad little, doomed cock of yours and those pathetic little berries you call balls. You’re going to strip and I’m going to giggle at your scrawny, naked body as you construct our little toy here. Step-by-step, you’re going to build the very machine that will destroy you. I’m going to have my one last night of fun with you then cut your cock and balls off leaving you as a non-gendered person for the rest of your life and there is nothing you can do to stop me.”

“Yes, mistress.” I said.

Jenna giggled slightly with a sensual, "God, that's so sexy. The thought of you flopping around in agony on the ground as your severed little cock lays bleeding but…" Her face turned flush as she whimpered slightly saying "I must be patient. The chance to castrate a man is a once in a lifetime opportunity for me and I'm going to savor every second of it. I'm recording tonight's session, by the way, I'll be rubbing my hard little clit watching you submit to my orders one final time, even shoving your cock under a guillotine which will drop that shiny, razor-sharp blade across it for years to come. That's quite a thought for you, isn't it? I will be squirting my womanly juices all over my bedsheets thinking about how I finally killed you as a man long after the last vestiges of testosterone have died within your body, and you shrivel up like an asexual monk."

My heart pounded in my chest in terror and anticipation as I replied, "that is… exciting."

"Take your shirt off." Jenna commanded. I quickly and silently obeyed, grabbing my t-shirt and sliding it up over my head. Her eyes glistened as she stared at my pale, skinny body. Somewhere out there, some other guy must have gotten my second dose of puberty because I sure as hell never received it. She licked her lips hungrily as she continued "take off your pants."

She leaned back in the chair and continued masturbating as I obediently stripped my slacks off from around my waist letting them fall to a pile on the floor before kicking them away. I stood in my underwear shivering under the watchful gaze of my goddess. Her lips parted into a sinister smile as she continued "take off your underwear...slowly. Let me see the cock that I'm going to murder tonight."

Just being in her presence had given me an erection. Shyly I looked down and to the side, unable to stare my goddess in the face, as I slowly lowered my boxer shorts feeling my cock stretch against the hem for a moment before springing free. I closed my eyes and shuddered as I felt the last vestiges of my clothing slide down across my knees and down my legs landing in a useless, crumpled heap on the floor.

"Oh god, I love that." Jenna said as she panted out in ecstasy. Her lips drew back into a sneer as she continued "you are whimpering and looking away while you hesitantly unveil your body to me. You strip like a rape victim undressing for her abuser. It's so fucking sexy how pathetic you are." She shook her head and giggled as she taunted "Do you even know you can just turn the fucking computer off and throw my machine in the trash?" She cocked an eyebrow before chuckling, "or did I break that part of your brain a long time ago?"

I held my silence. I knew these were rhetorical questions and her answer came soon enough as she spoke for me saying "we both know you're powerless to do anything other than exactly as I command."

"Yes, mistress." I replied quietly.

"look at me." She commanded.

I turned and looked into the screen directly as a smug smile spread across her face.

She pulled her hand out from her shorts and licked her fingers saying, "mmhmm my womanhood is getting wet just thinking of what I'm going to do to you tonight. I always enjoy seeing your sad little cock and pathetic little body. But you've never even seen the body of the woman who enjoys torturing you every Friday. Right? You've never seen me naked."

"That's correct, mistress." I replied. Sure, she normally wore skimpy outfits and every time she tortured me, she masturbated to the session herself until wetness would spread across the bottom of her shorts, but I have never actually seen her body beneath her clothes. She continued "I'm going to show it to you tonight. You're going to look right at the tits you'll never touch and the pussy you'll never fill. You're going to watch me squirting in orgasm while that steel blade slices your little giblets off and leaves them in a neat little bloody pile so that you will never orgasm again. Sound exciting?"

I gasped and replied "yes, mistress."

"Good. Now, we'll be turning that sad little cock and ball of yours into a pussy and the boys do like it when a girl like you shaves her pussy, so go fetch some clippers or a razor. You're going to give me a nice, clean view of you carving all those disgusting, scraggly hairs off your cock, balls, and crotch. Remember to do a good job, you're preparing your manhood for its funeral. I want your cock and balls shaved, clean, and as pretty as they will ever be when I devour them with my steel blade."

I went to the bathroom and, after some digging around, returned with a pair of electric clippers. "Good boy, now get your sad little cock and balls up close to the camera so I can make sure you shave well."

I plugged the clippers in to a nearby outlet and turned them on releasing a buzz. My hand shook lightly as I stood there in front of the computer silently running the clippers down one side of my crotch cutting a path of pale flesh beneath my curly pubic hairs. Jenna spoke, even though I couldn't see her well from my current angle as I had angled the camera to look at my crotch. She said, "Nice. This should help you get used to your new role in life, that of a shaved and weak little eunuch."

I shaved in silence for a while before Jenna said.
"Jordan?"

"Yes, mistress?" I said as I continued shaving my crotch for her.

"Do you think you could ever get an alpha man to be your boyfriend?"

"I…I… I never…"

"Don't be shy. Just answer the question."

"I never thought about it before, Mistress." I answered.

"Mumm… maybe I'll send you one last present. A bottle of HRT to get you started on your transition from pathetic boy to hot bitch. That would be a funny thought, you growing a pair of breasts and finding yourself bent over a couch as a hot, powerful alpha male fucks your ass from behind. Maybe you'll learn how to suck cock like a good little girl. Just think, Jordan, this might be the best thing to ever happen to you in this life."

"I…I don't know if I can be with a man that way, mistress."

"Oh, I think you'll make a fine little girl, Jordan. But first, let's destroy this sad little manhood of yours. Lift that tiny little cock of yours and let me see you shave those cute little berry balls for me." I did as she instructed lifting my cock and holding it back with my left hand as I gingerly ran the clippers over my scrotum with my right hand. The sensation of buzzing blades dicing thousands of times per second mere millimeters away from my testes thrilled me with the taste of danger while the knowledge that I was merely shaving them to cut them off rendered the terror moot. Jenna cooed as she watched saying "there you go, yes, shave all those nasty hairs off my new balls there. Make them sweet, clean, and pretty for my steel machine. Just thing, Jordan, you'll finally get to penetrate something. You're going to slide that little cock of yours into my guillotine and make my brutal slicing machine your very first and very last girlfriend. Lucky boy, you get to lose your virginity and your sexuality tonight."

"Thank you, mistress." I panted out as my whole body tensed at the thrill and fear of anticipation. This drew a deluge of giggles from her lips followed by "now shave your cock for me, I still see some scraggly little hairs around its base. I did as she instructed feeling the whirring machine slice with maniacal speed at the fine pubic hairs around my cock. Little tremors of pain sprung up like drops scattering across a glassy-smooth pond as the clipper occasionally pinched and pulled at my hairs rather than cutting them. I winced and my goddess asked, "cut yourself?"

"No, just…pinched some hair."

"Good. I do want my cock and balls to be fully intact when you ship them to me."

"Ship them to you?"

"Yes, after you cut your manhood off, you'll plunk it in a jar of alcohol and mail it to me."

My eyes grew glassy, and a smile spread across my face as I whispered "You… want my cock?"

She smiled at me warmly saying "Jordan, it will be my most cherished trophy. A reminder of how I took everything from you, and you helped me do it. Every time I look at your severed cock, I'll remember you as you are now, a pathetic little pain slut, with a broken mind just begging to be abused by mommy."

"Yes, mistress." I replied.

"Good boy. Now take the laptop with you to your bathroom. Set it up where I can see you with your cock dangling over the sink." I gingerly picked up my laptop and stepped over to the bathroom. The world outside the crystal-clear glow of the electronic device seemed dismal and grey. My mind-numbing and humiliating dead-end job, my extortionate rent, my eternally disappointed parents… somehow the glow of my goddess commanding me to commit acts of self-mutilation pushed back those dark clouds of existential decay as the promise of a brave and exciting life as an adult degraded into the bland monotony of 'adulting.'

I set the laptop on the toilet top aiming it towards the bathroom sink. "Good boy. Now wash my cock and balls for me in your sink there. Use lots of warm water and soap." I grabbed up the bar of soap and turned the water on asking "hot or warm?"

"Just warm." Goddess commanded. She swallowed and said, "this is not part of your torture. Just…" She sighed and continued, "keeping down the chance of infection. Although it would be fun to kill you, I promised myself that I would leave you alive after tonight so, unfortunately, we need to make a few accommodations to accomplish that."

As the warm water cascaded over the purple tip of my manhood and I rubbed white hand-soap across my shaft I said "it… really would be okay if you killed me tonight." I looked at the screen and she stared back into my eyes as I washed my cock in front of her. Her face turned slightly sad, and she took this in thoughtfully as she continued, "from this day forward, for the rest of your life, I want you to remember this, Jordan. Your heart beats…"

She lowered her voice and continued, "…because I am cruel. I won't let you enjoy the mercy of death tonight. I'm ruining the act of dying for you same as I ruin your orgasms. Your life is my final act of sadism against you."

I can never explain the thought process that brought a smile to my face at her words. "Thank you, mistress."

"For leaving you alive and miserable?"

I shook my head and said, "for making my life…something. Everyone and everything else remind me every day that my life is…nothing."

"Shhh…shhh… Jordan. Remember, it isn't any fun for me if I'm not the one hurting you."

"I know, I know, mistress. I just…" I sighed as I continued washing my balls and said "I just wanted to let you know that the only part of my week that I look forward to is Friday night. You honestly enjoy hurting me. No one else on this planet even cares that I exist. The only time I feel special, the only time that I feel wanted, is when you are torturing me." I choked up a bit and sniffed back a sob as I continued "thank you for hurting me."

"Oh, fuck, you're going to make me cry." Jenna complained as she wiped tears away from her eyes. She gritted her teeth and went off script as she continued softly, "that's not very goddess-mistress of me."

"You've been honest with me. I'll be honest with you." Jenna continued as her face contorted slightly. She leaned in close to the computer on her side saying, "Jordan, I'm fucking terrified."

"Terrified of what?"

"What if the baby inside me, is a boy? Jordan, oh-fucking-shit, what if I have a son?" Jenna gasped out fearfully.

I squinted at her, and she continued "I'm a god-damn menace to mankind, Jordan. You can't see it, because you're clamped in my jaws, but…oh, fuck… a baby boy… growing up under the care of a …what… a sadistic sociopath like me? I can control any man, but what if I can't control myself?"

I thought about this for a moment before replying, "I think…I hope… your relationship with him will be different than the one you have with me."

This seemed to calm her down a bit as she sat back in the chair and breathed out a sigh. "Oh, fuck, Jordan. I really can't make up my mind as to whether to murder you out of pure mercy for saying something so kind or try and schedule a call next week as a depraved act of selfish greed. I suppose I can split the difference between those two possibilities and split your balls instead."

I turned the water off and patted my manhood dry with a towel saying, "they are nice and clean for you."

"Good boy. Now it's time for you to construct that sweet little machine of mine which will destroy your manhood. Bring the laptop back out to your room."

I did as she commanded and set the laptop down on the desk angling it to look at me. "I suppose this part is rather boring, and I hate for us to get bored, so I'll make you a deal."

"A deal?" I asked.

"More like a game. Something to help pass the time while you construct the machine. For each part you put on, I'll take an article of clothing off."

My eyes went wide, and Jenna giggled. "Exciting?"

"I… I…"

"Speechless?" She taunted.

I swallowed hard and asked, "you'll actually do that?"

"I already told you that you were going to see me naked tonight."

"I know it's just…"

I looked up into the screen to see a concerned look on her face as I continued "I just got so used to you hurting and humiliating me, It just feels…wrong… somehow."

I bowed my head and whispered "sorry, Mistress."

"Jordan, look at me."

To my shock, Jenna had removed her pink blouse and her perky little tits glistened in the light of the room. Her perfectly rounded, smooth areolas had cute, glinting nipples poking up in excitement from them. She caressed her breasts with her hands and cupped them gently smiling at me.

"Does it hurt knowing you'll never touch these?" She asked.

I stared at her breasts for a while before breathily replying "yes."

"Good boy." She said. She sighed as she looked down at her breasts saying "in nine-months I'll be feeding a baby with these. They'll swell up like balloons and the moment the little one weens; they'll collapse like an overcooked souffle." Her eyes turned sad as she said, "both of us are running out of time. Baby-fat, mommy-hair, haggard stare…" She muttered these as her eyes grew distant and trembled on the edge of tears as she looked back up into my face saying "Jason may still fuck me from time-to-time but tonight may be my last night that I can use my body to properly torture a man. Your goddess is powerful, but she isn't eternal."

She swallowed hard and looked down at her breasts as she squeezed them in her hands saying "at least they are pretty for now. I suppose I got a bit ahead of myself on our game here, already topless and you haven't built anything. That box should have an Allen key, fish it out and attach those sturdy steel rails onto the machine that you're going to fuck."

I did as instructed, finding the appropriate bolts and fasteners. Despite its brutality, the machine seemed rather simple and straightforward to construct. I even smiled a bit at how easily everything fit together.

"Is it a bit of fun, working with your hands like this?" Jenna asked.

"It is, actually."

"Well, you'll still have that after today." Jenna said calmly. As I mounted the stand into place, Jenna stood up and slid her spandex shorts off revealing crinkly-looking black lingerie panties.

"Is that what you always wear underneath?" I asked in surprise.

"Of course. These panties…mmmhmmm" Jenna moaned lights as she ran her hands along her hips shifting them back and forth before slipping her fingers underneath the hem of her panties saying "give me confidence boost I need sometimes. Do you like seeing me in them?"

"Yes." I breathily replied.

"As you slide that blade which will chop your sad little cock off up into place, I'll slide down these panties so you can see the pussy you never got to enjoy."

I kept my eyes on the screen as I lifted the blade into place, careful not to lose a finger in the process. I watched in awe as Jenna slowly slid the black lingerie panties down across her hips exposing more of her smooth, flawless crotch until she got to her perfectly shaved pussy where two, delicious-looking pouty little labial lips met in a sweet kiss of her womanhood. From this point she quickly dropped the panties past her knees and kicked them off her ankles as I clicked the blade into its locking latch. She stood back a bit so I could see her whole body in the frame of my computer. She spread her legs open about a shoulder width apart and lifted her arms up sliding her hands in behind her head fluffing out her golden hair slightly and arching her back a bit spreading her warm, smooth breasts out in front of her as she thrust her hips forward giving me an unbelievable view of her womanhood. She posed like this and looked down at the computer screen as a smile spread across her face.

"Is my body everything you ever imagined it to be?"

"So much more. You're like a heavenly being of beauty and majesty."

She lowered her arms and put her hands on her widely spaced, beautifully effeminate hips as she replied "when I stand in the light of your eyes, Jordan, I feel like a heavenly being. I feel so powerful, like I can do anything. God, this power is as addictive to me as my sex is to you." She nodded towards the guillotine saying "last few parts to put on. You noticed the wall-plug by now, for sure."

"I did. That and a USB cable" I said scrounging up the correct parts.

She nodded saying "Good, plug the machine into the wall and plug the USB cable to your laptop."

"I never knew a guillotine to work electrically before." I said as I dutifully plugged it in.

"This is a very special machine. You remember those bands and the spreader from before?"

"Yes."

"Use the spreader to put those bands on the pegs on both the front and back of the retaining plate. Right around where your manhood goes."

I did as instructed, spreading the powerful elastic bands around the same hole I was going to stick my dick into shortly.

"Thanks for your patience with these minor conveniences, Jordan. It's all because I've decided to keep you alive." Jenna sat down at the computer at her end, and I watched as she typed something while looking at something else on the screen. I jumped in terror as the blade sliced downward and the pegs on the retaining plate retracted back snapping the bands into place on either side with a sickening steel ringing sound. The entire process took less than a few milliseconds and my eyes went wide with terror as Jenna's eyes went wide with excitement.

"Oh, fuck, yes, it actually works." She said with a gleeful chuckle in her throat. She panted in excitement like a little girl learning she's going to receive a pony for her birthday as she said to me "I really am going to castrate you tonight. Oh, my god, I was so scared this wouldn't work. This is fucking amazing, I can input the remote commands, just press 'enter' and off your cock goes."

Her shoulders lifted almost to her ears as she shivered in anticipation. She licked her lips and said "Oh, my god, I get to fucking murder your cock and balls. This is so amazing." She bit her lower lip briefly before blowing out a sigh saying "go ahead and reset the machine, Jordan. Now you know how it works. I hope it feels just as real to you as it does to me now."

It did. My hands shook as I carefully slid the heavy metal blade back up the rails to lock it back into place. As it slid into the lock, the metal pegs protruded once more from the retaining plate. The world seemed to spin around me as my vision tunneled in on the hole my cock would soon be inside as I mounted a veterinary-grade castration band around it.

“Good boy, now have a seat in your chair.”

I collapsed into it, my head spiraling with emotions.

“You okay, Jordan?” Jenna asked sounding concerned.

“Yeah, just…” I panted in a mix of anticipation and fear.

“Jordan, it’s okay, I’m here with you.” She said. I looked at the screen see Jenna’s smiling face. My focus and my mind seemed to crystallize around her, and I realized my mistake earlier which had nearly led to my downfall. I had thought about what I wanted, what was going to happen to me, how I thought my life should be. None of that mattered because I don’t matter. All that matters is her, Jenna. In the face of that goddess, I am nothing more than meat to be toyed with and tortured and should behave as such. A smile spread across my face as I whispered back, “thank you, Jenna.”

She leaned back a bit and shimmied her breasts letting her nipples wave back and forth invitingly as she giggled asking “after all these years, are you finally ready to have sex?”

I nodded. She said, “slide the machine onto the chair with you. Just rest it in front of you for now.” I had to use both hands to life the heavy device down onto the plain wooden chair along with me. Seeing it fully constructed and knowing what it was capable of gave me a pause and I eyed Jenna nervously as she leaned into her screen to watch.

“Good boy. Now, slowly, slide your cock into that hole of death. Slide it in sweet and deep same as if that hole was my body.”

My cock trembled and I held onto the base of the machine as I looked up fearfully at the blade which dangled from the electronic lock.

"Don't worry, Jordan, I won't cut your dick off until you are fully inside the machine and I'm ready to do so." Jenna said reassuringly.

Cold steel greeted my frenulum as I slowly slid my cock in through the hole in the plated. Nothing but cold air greeted it on the other side and yet my body quivered with anticipation as Jenna moaned.

"Ohh.... Good boy. Yes, press your cock into the machine which will castrate you at the flick of my finger. Like a sad little child getting the stick from the backyard that mommy is going to beat him with, do your part to help me murder your manhood." Jenna taunted sensually. She continued, "Here, I'll help you."

She sat back on the couch and put her legs up on either side of the laptop such that she straddled it giving me a full view of her crotch and sweet breasts. She reached down one hand and pressed her lithe fingers against her pussy spreading it open letting me see the beautifully perfect little pink triangular lips inside just above her wet and deliciously tight hole. "Imagine your sticking your cock into my body as you go."

Instead of looking at the machine which would soon kill my manhood, I stared at the body of the woman who would soon trigger it. I gasped and sighed as I pressed my cock in fully to the retention plate feeling the cold metal press against my freshly shaved and sensitive balls. The metal support posts on the front side of the machine slid up under my buttocks cradling me into place against the back of the seat. The disturbing realization that I could not escape this machine activating if I wanted to blended with the revelation that I wouldn't want to escape its clean, surgical removal of my unnecessary body parts.

"Ohh... that got your dick nice and hard. Just think of all that throbbing blood inside it that will no longer be yours once I slice it off you." Jenna giggled coyly as she reached down with her other hand and began caressing her clit. "I want to see you shove those sweet little balls of yours into my nasty little machine. I can't wait to see them pop through to the other side so I can pop them off your body."

It took me a few tries but using my hand I was able to pinch the skin on my scrotum and slip one ball through the plate followed by the other. With this done, my body now sat in two halves. The larger half of my normal body, arms, face, legs, torso…all the parts I got to keep after tonight and the smaller, yet equally important half of my cock and balls, all of my sex organs and manhood lay across the gulf of the steel plate with separated me from my doomed and vulnerable sex organs. I shuddered as I looked into the eyes of the woman who could cut my entire manhood off at the touch of a button.

She pushed a few buttons on the computer on her side saying, "don't touch the blade from this point forward."

"Why?"

"I'm turning the heater on. It will be nice and searing hot when it comes down now. Should cauterize and seal your manhood neatly.

She continued typing something onto the computer.

"What are you doing now?" I asked as I sat there with my cock mounted in the device and the terrifying steel blade trembling on the verge of my castration. Jenna's eyes were wide with delight as she fiddled about on the computer on her end saying, "I'm screen-shotting this." She clicked and a smile spread across her face "Oh, god, that's so fucking sexy. Seeing you there with your sad little junk in my slicing machine. This is going to be my fucking wallpaper, I know it. I'm going to be jilling off to this picture of you for years." Her eyes flickered up to meet mine as her smile turned cute and she continued "Jordan, I've been dreaming about this moment ever since I caught you staring at my breasts back in seventh grade. Say goodbye to your manhood. I'm finally going to go all the way and cut every part of you off so it can rot and die. You'll never have a hard-on or any on for the rest of your life and it will all be because of me."

Painful logic tortured my mind. Disturbing thoughts of pulling my dick out from her machine, turning off the computer, maybe trying to talk to that chubby girl in accounting who I might actually have a chance with… what if… what if…? What if there was more to life than worshiping a goddess who talked openly about murdering me and was about to destroy my ability to ever enjoy sex again? The question roiled deep emotions within me, and the turmoil made my soul grow weak and my worship feel blasphemous under these illicit thoughts.

I trembled and a tear rolled down my cheek. I sucked back a sob as I stared at the heavy steel blade which would soon part me from my manhood.

"Shhh…" Jordan shushed over the screen. An ominous smile spread across her face as she asked in a passionate tone, "Remember that you love me."

"I've loved you since high school." I said.

"And you realize you'll never have me, right? Look at that tiny thing, even fully erect your cock isn't even half the size of my husband's. I mean, look at this pussy."

She leaned back and spread her legs reaching down and stretching open her delicious, pink lips with her fingers.

Tears fell from my eyes as I nodded. I couldn't tell if they were tears of pain, remorse, or relief. Some deep, primal part of our souls seemed to meet in that moment. She leaned in close to the screen on her side and continued "then you should be happy to end your ability to breed for me."

I shuddered and she continued, "you're never going to get a chance to use those body parts on a woman. The only thing they will bring you is disappointment and pain. You know that to be true, right?"

I nodded.

She continued, "You should sacrifice those parts to me. You were never really a man, and deep down inside a part of you understands that."

I nodded.

"Good little boy, Jordan. You ready?

I nodded.

She smiled sweetly and said, "We're going to fuck now. This is going to be actual sex. No ruined orgasm. No denial. This is going to be a good, nice, proper, fuck. Do you understand?"

"Yes, mistress."

"Start jerking off… slowly." She cocked her head to the side and cupped one breast in her left hand while her right hand spread her labia open, and she strummed her clit. She moaned saying "Enjoy it, Jordan. I know you've been dreaming of fucking me your entire life and tonight, I'm going to let you do it. This is one last night for you to dream. I'm going to make your dreams come true and then I'm going to end your dreams for all eternity. Dream big, Jordan. Dream that we're back in high school again…"

I moaned in pleasure and Jenna warned, "ohh… don't cum yet, Jordan. This will be the last fuck you ever have. Savor it. Make it last. When you release, I want you to spray cum all over the image of my hot, delicious fucking body on the computer screen in front of you. I want it to be a lot, Jordan. I want it to be every fucking drop of cum you ever dreamed of squirting into my lithe, sweet little body. This will be the last sperm you ever produce and you're going to spray it all over me on your computer here. You're going to sacrifice your seed to this goddess."

"Yes, goddess." I panted out.

"It's high school again… you asked me to prom but this time, this time Jordan, I say 'yes.'" Jenna spoke aloud in fantasy as her body trembled with the force of her own growing orgasm. I felt my fingers caressing the head of my cock same as I felt the hard, cold steel plate cradling my balls just on the other side of the guillotine where the parts of my body which would soon no longer be mine lay. It felt like these pieces of me now lived in a distant land and yet the sensation of pleasure from the touch of my fingers felt all too real as it resonated with Jenna's words spoken directly into my mind and soul.

"I'm wearing a thin, strapless white cotton dress with my hair all up in a stylish little updo tied with a ribbon. You're wearing some suit jacket borrowed from your uncle or whatever. We're on the dance floor slow-dancing and you feel my lithe little hand come up between your legs. Excitement grows in your heart as my fingers find your cock but instead of massaging it, I slide my hand further back wrapping my fingers around your balls." Jenna said as she continued fingering herself. She moaned and said, "I squeeze your little balls right there on the dance floor. Squeeze your balls for me, Jordan." Obediently, I stopped jacking off and slid my hand down squeezing my own balls feeling the pressure and pain well up across my entire body at the torment.

"I pull you in close as you realize that you're powerless, only my sense of mercy is the only thing keeping me from crushing your balls to mush between my fingers. I whisper into your ear 'come home with me, so I can fuck, torture, castrate, and murder you.' What do you say, Jordan? What would you have said to such an offer back during high school prom?"

"Yes, mistress."

"Oh, you wouldn't have called me 'mistress' back then, Jordan. Squeeze your balls a little harder as punishment for making such a stupid mistake." I tightened my grip and whimpered at the pain emanating from my crotch.

"Yes… Jenna." I said.

"Good boy, release your balls. I let them go and we continue to dance as you weakly lean against me. You're whimpering in pain through the slow dance. You don't know what scares you more. Going home with me or going home without me."

I released my tight grip on my balls gasping in relief as I did so.

Jenna moaned saying "oh, god, it's so fucking hot that you're powerless to stop me." Jenna rolled her head casually and smiled saying, "I like you like this, Jordan. Weak, pathetic, like a sad little worm that I'm pinning down to a cork-board ready to yield up your soft little flesh to my blade as I watch you open, pull out your insides, and let you die. If only I appreciated the power that I had over, you back in high school. I just didn't realize my strength. I could have done whatever the fuck I wanted to do to you. That's what I regret, Jordan. Not that I kicked you, but that I didn't take you to prom, make you my boyfriend, and lived out my dreams to torture you horrifically every single night." Her breath stuttered as she continued "I could see it now, the night before graduation, I take you up to my room and cut your cock off. I would then spend the rest of the night kissing your lips sweetly as you bleed to death. Oh, god, I wouldn't even have to tie you up. You wouldn't have even whimpered a word of protest. I could have murdered you slowly and brutally. Like a good little boy, you would have just laid there quietly and let me do it to you as well."

I trembled as she spoke. She gasped and panted at her own fantasy as she continued "go ahead and start jerking off again. It's better late than never, I suppose. I'll cut your cock off you now and, just like a good little boy, you're not going to do anything to stop me. The fact that you could just slide your balls and cock right out of my machine there hasn't even crossed your submissive little mind and that dedication to being devoured and destroyed by me is even hotter than when my big, powerful husband pushes my ankles up past my ears, chokes my slender little neck, and spits in my mouth when he power-fucks my little body."

Jenna shuddered and continued.

"So, it is prom again. Your dreams are coming true, Jordan. After getting ball-squeezed on the dance floor in front of the entire school, I'm taking you home. My parents are out of town and you're finally getting to go home with a girl. The night air is cold as you quietly sit in the passenger seat of that old Honda I had back in high school.

You watch me slide into the driver's seat and I tell you to put your seatbelt on. I grab the side of your face and smile at you saying that you're not allowed to get hurt, unless I'm the one hurting you. What do you say?"

"I nod quietly and put my seatbelt on." I replied.

"Good boy. We drive back to my place, it's dark and we're alone. You hold my hand and I turn on the lights as we go inside. You can't help but stare at my body even as we stop by the kitchen, and I pull out a knife from the block to torture and kill you with. It's not a big, impressive butchers knife, rather a razor sharp, thin, paring knife. The kind I would normally cut vegetables with. I pull you in close and wrap my hand around your waist while wrapping my other around your neck. You feel me press the flat of the blade gently against your neck as I passionately kiss you. You feel cold steel against your vulnerable throat and my hot lips against yours as I press my warm little body tight against yours before releasing the kiss and whispering into your ear "ready to suffer and die for me, my good little boy?"

"Yes." I whispered back to her.

Jenna shuddered and began stumming her clit even harder.

"Where should I kill you, Jordan? The kitchen, or my bedroom?"

I panted, nearing orgasm myself as I whispered back "the kitchen."

Jenna smiled saying "good idea. Blood is a bitch to clean out of carpet. Besides, no one is home, no one is going to see us, no one is going to hear you scream. You can't save yourself, my power over your mind is too strong. You're nothing but a helpless victim now with nothing to do but find out what I do to you next."

Jenna tipped her head back and her leg began shaking as she whimpered out "god, I wish I could be there in person. Hold your soft, pathetic balls in the palm of my hand and feel my blade bite into them as you whimper and cry. You about to cum?"

"Yes." I replied honestly.

"slap your balls."

I did as instructed feeling the crushing pain emanating upwards from my crotch into my chest.

"Harder!" She shouted and I slapped once more groaning in pain and jiggling the machine which trembled on the edge of castrating me.

"Good boy. You can jerk off again, but slow… I want to enjoy my time with you. I would have enjoyed my time with you back in school too. I place one hand against your chest and gently push you backwards holding the knife in my other hand. You feel the kitchen table compress against your buttocks and realize I'm forcing you to lay down on it. Once you're on the old, oaken table, I climb up as well. You see me towering over you as I hike my dress up and straddle across your crotch letting you feel the warmth of my pussy through your pants and my panties. I pull the ribbon out of my hair and tell you to hold your hands out to me. You do so and I tie the lace-fringed pink little ribbon around your wrists in many tight, little knots. You watch in confusion as I push your hands up over your head, doing this brings me closer to you. Our faces are so close that we can almost kiss, but I don't kiss you this time, rather I lay the flat of the blade against your cheek, just beneath your staring eyeball. I say 'I know you've been feasting on my body with these disgusting, perverted eyes for years. There's no use denying it. I would love to cut them out of your skull, but I also want you to see what I do to your sad little body. Like I broke my Barbie doll, you're nothing more than a toy for me to break.' I then slide the knife down along your neck until I come to your shirt. Here, I let the blade bite into the button knots and fabric carving your shirt open destroying your clothes but not ruining your body just yet. You watch me as I sit back up and slide back a bit continuing to carve through your clothes splitting them open leaving your bare, pale flesh at my mercy. I unbuckle your belt and then open your pants before sliding my blade beneath the hem of your underwear. You feel the cold steel glinting along your hard little cock for a moment before I violently slash outwards ripping your underwear open and releasing your cock to come out to meet the girl of its dreams only to realize that nightmares are dreams too."

I groaned as she moaned. We were both near orgasm and I could tell it. Some strange part of me could almost begin to forget the guillotine contraption my manhood lay locked inside of awaiting its horrible fate. She continued "you watch as I stand up over you, my legs spread over your thighs and my head nearly touching the ceiling standing on the table like that. You stare in awe as I strip off my dress letting my hot, powerful, sensual body come out so I can use it to increase my control over you and magnify your pain. Like a lioness crouching over its prey, I crouch grabbing hold of your cock in my hand, guiding it into my sweet, delicious, tight, wet pussy." Jenna began shuddering and her hips started instinctively thrusting at this point as I felt my own desire and sexuality begin to grow as the pain from my earlier ball-slaps subsided.

"I bounce up and down on your cock a bit, letting you feel the delicious, sweet, powerful sexual pleasure my body has to offer but I stop short of bringing you to orgasm. I slide the sweet little knife up and you watch in awe and terror as I bring the point of it to your slender little belly. You try sucking in to avoid the blade, but it's no use, this time, I am going to cut you. You feel the heat of my pussy around your cock and the cold sting of the blade as I slice a thin line into the right-hand side of your belly."

Jenna gave a nearly orgasmic giggle as she continued "are you going to stop me, Jordan?"

"No." I reply.

"Oh, it's so fucking easy to control you mind, body and soul. God, I could have lived out my fantasies with you when I was in high school. I continue, rivulets of warm blood pool along your abdomen and stream down your sides onto the table as I keep cutting you. Thin, petite little slices, first a vertical one, then a horizontal one, then four of them next to those at angles, then two small angle ones and alternating small angle ones." She shuddered and continued "any time you start to lose your wood from the pain, I stop cutting and give you a few thrusts feeling your pathetic little cock barely pierce my wet pussy. It's not wet because we're fucking, it's wet because I'm living out my dreams with your body. I continue cutting and fucking you and, before you know it, I've now decorated your belly. You have the word 'LOSER' carved across your belly in all capital letters. I grab your head and pull it up so you can see my handy work. You watch your belly bleed as I thrust against you again asking if you are afraid of other people seeing what I did to you. Are you, Jordan? Are you afraid of the boys and girls in the school making fun of you for having your belly carved up by a girl?"

"No."

"Correct answer. You know why you shouldn't be afraid?"

"Because it is meant to happen. You're my goddess and I'm your worshiper."

"Wrong answer."

Jenna giggled saying "wrong answer Jordan. The reason you shouldn't be afraid of other kids laughing at you when you go back to school is because you're not going back to school. You're not going to do next week's math homework assignment. You're not going to chat with your friends or graduate or do any of those things because I'm going to murder you tonight. You're going to die here, between the legs of a woman. Where most life begins, yours is going to end. Are you scared, Jordan? Are you going to fight back? Run away? Anything?"

"No, goddess."

"Good answer. It's time to end this, Jordan. I can't hold out any longer. I slide the blade down and slip it in between our crotches. You feel your cock deep inside my pussy while the hard steel blade rests just alongside it. I have a strong grasp on the blade as I pin you down with my other hand. You see the blood pooling away from your belly, spreading red, cloying matte across our bodies and realize the reason I cut you was to weaken you up a bit, make you easier to kill. I continue to fuck you. Your belly burns in anguish as your cock dances in heaven. I whisper your future to you saying "once you cum inside me, I'll cut your dick right off. I'm going to take it all the way into my pussy. I'm going to feel this sad little thing swallowed right into my womanhood and feel it shrivel and die inside my pussy as you lay here bleeding to death on my kitchen table like a good little boy who knows when it's his time to go. Ready?"

"Yes." I said.

Jenna smiled as her body shook uncontrollably as she said "I'm going to count down from three. Spray cum all over your laptop, and I'll finally slice that cock and balls right off your fucking body."

Her voice turned serious as she counted down.

"One…

Two…

Three."

I groaned as ecstatic pleasure overwhelmed my body. My balls tensed against the steel plate as my cock sprayed cum all over the laptop keyboard and screen. At the same time, Jenna shuddered and howled in her own orgasm squirting womanly juices all over the couch she sat on. For a moment in time, we danced there in pure joy together across the gulf of the internet. Passion and power flowed through my body as I shuddered in orgasmic delight watching sticky ropes of cum splatter against my laptop, desk, and floor. I don't know why, but I never cum quite as much when I'm not being dominated or tortured. After the delicious delight of orgasm, my breathing began to slow as my cock weakly pressed out the final drops of cum which drizzled from my purple tipped head. Jenna whimpered as her body shook and her pussy lips looked like they contracted and stretched hungrily all on their own. She looked down and our eyes met. A smile spread across her face as tears thinly dripped from the corners of her large, beautiful eyes.

I shuddered in post nut clarity as I watched her lift a long, beautiful leg, slide her small, bare foot sweetly in front of the screen, and push her big toe down on the keyboard with a cruel smile spread across her face.

My mind didn't register the sensation at first, only her words as she said, "I hope it was as good for you as it was for me" rang in my ears. In the next moment, my crotch exploded with agony the likes of which I had never experienced before as my chest compressed and I slumped forward hugging the very self-same machine which had just castrated me completely. I heard a sickening *plop* sound and looked down to see that the burning hot steel had sliced right through my cock and balls like they were butter as a tension band snapped into place compressing my stump while my manhood plopped down onto the edge of the chair on the other side held together with its own little tension band. The world spiraled around me as shock set in and I distantly heard Jenna calling my name from the computer.

I looked up with my mouth cocked open and my eyes blurred over. I tried to suck in a breath, but my body wouldn't breath. She stared at me the way a woman would look at a sunset over a lake or a piece of art as she whispered, "god, you're so fucking beautiful." She didn't break eye contact as she said, "breathe in Jordan." Together, we drew in a deep breath, and she instructed "breathe out." My body could no longer obey me, but some ingrained instinct allowed it to obey her, and, in that moment, she controlled my breathing as tingling sensations of disgust and horror trickled their way up my spine and danced sickeningly across my flesh. My eyes grew heavy, and nausea overtook my stomach as the pain exceeded beyond the sensation and started to manifest in other ways. I gagged as my body shuddered and I felt my heart grip tight in my chest like it had been filled with concrete. Some strange trickling thoughts danced about in the back, logical recesses of my mind that had avoided the system-wide shutdown, which I seemed to be going through. The irony that, despite her provisions to keep me alive, I would still die from shock and blood-loss was not lost on me. I supposed that's what I deserved, and I prayed that, in the future, Jenna could find a stronger, better worshipper than myself. Someone who can endure a castration without dying like some pathetic little beta-boy like me. The world darkened and my body grew weak as I heard Jenna's voice rise from consolation to screams of terror.

Somehow in the realms of the damned, I suppose, I heard a deep male voice shouting, "You fucking pieces-of-shit whore! You fucking killed him! The only reason… the only fucking reason, bitch! That I let you keep whoring on the web and fucking with these beta-losers is the god-damn money. And now, you fucking mailed a god damn cock-cutted to one of your bitch-boys and killed the fucker. That's fucking lot-lizard bitch thinking there from a piece of fucking trailer-park-trash-barbie with more tits and ass than brains. Why the fuck did I marry you? You useless fucking whore!"

"No! Please! It was an accident! I didn't mean-" Jenna pleaded.

I heard a loud slapping sound followed by Jenna's screaming and a struggle. I lulled my head up to see Jenna, still naked, pinned under a burly, bearded man in a sleeveless white tank-top and tattered jeans as he choked her. Tears streamed from her eyes which bulged out from her face as he let go of her neck to slap her across her face hard. His blow turned her head forcing her to look into the screen. We locked eyes as I gingerly picked myself up off the floor where I lay next to the now toppled over guillotine and my own severed cock. She gurgled and pointed at me urgently as he cocked back a fist to punch her hard in the face.

"Live…he-uh-uh…live…" She choked out. The man, I assume it was her husband Jason, turned his head to look at me where I lay on the ground.

"Shear fucking luck, bitch. Still, I'm going to learn your whore-ass a lesson you won't ever forget." He made to punch her as I weakly reached out mentally pleading with him to stop but nowhere near strong or vocal enough to give voice my protest.

She raised a hand to stop him and pleaded "Please…don't kill me…our baby…" Jason paused and sneered at her before lowering his fist. He threw her down on the ground saying "Lucky you're knocked up, whore. Otherwise, I would make it look like a fucking accident."

My mouth hung open limply in shock as Jenna lay in a crumpled heap on the ground sobbing.

"Oh...fuck." I muttered.

"For god's fucking sake, Jordan, don't look at me." She pleaded. She curled up on the floor in front of the couch and hugged her knees. She peered over her kneecaps at me. The fact that her pussy peeked out from between her feet didn't even register in my mind as I was too fixated on her swollen left eye. "I don't want you to see me like this. I never wanted you to see me like this." She whimpered.

"I thought you were…"

"I lied."

"But… the…"

"Lies! Jordan, Fucking lies, every fucking part of it…" She seethed out bitterly. Her eyes darted to where Jason had just left and then back to me as she continued "except for the baby… and… my husband-er-fucking monster that I'm trapped with." She growled out as she wiped away a tear before wincing in pain at touching her beaten face.

"Goddess?" I whispered.

"I'm no goddess, Jordan. I have no magic. I have no power. Goddesses don't exist. All that exists is…" Jenna whimpered and continued "a beaten housewife desperate to feel special." Her face turned dreamy as she continued "the way you looked at me, the way I felt… important…powerful…" She lowered her face into her knees and cried, "it's all gone now."

My world splintered into a million parts in that moment. My mouth moved before my brain could.

"You should come here."

I couldn't believe the words from my lips. Somehow the thought crystallized. For the first time in my entire existence, I had something to offer to another person. Not some common things like a piece of bread or whatever but a real, life-changing, solution.

"Huh?" Jenna asked.

I looked into her beaten and beautiful face as I whispered, "does Jason know my address?" Her eyes darted nervously before she shook her head.

"Jenna… every time I was with you, I felt special, important, I felt…"

"Oh, fuck-off. You're just a horny simp hoping I'll bang him." She hissed back.

"Really?!" I shouted in reply pointing to the bloody stump on my crotch. She took the sight in before saying, "I suppose you have a point that you don't have a cock. But what if…"

I continued, "you'll be safe here. That's a lot more than you can say for where you are now."

Her eyes looked off distantly for a while before she whispered, "god fucking damn me." She dropped her head down saying, "who am I kidding? That bastard in the sky damned me a long time ago." She looked up at me saying "I won't leave my husband for another man. I made a vow and I never break my vows."

I nodded saying sadly, "I understand."

I stared down at the floor wishing that I could help her somehow.

"Which is why it's lucky that you're no longer a man."

I looked back up into the screen. A look of determination crossed her face as she said "I'll have to wait for him to fall asleep to get away. I'll be there before morning. No one, absolutely nobody is to know where I am. Do you understand?"

"Completely."

A soft smile crossed her face as she said, "I'll see you soon, Jordan."

Neutered By Network

The brisk, mid-October air fluttered through his shoulder-length, blonde hair as Adam stepped out from his car parked just outside the massive cinderblock and steel building which bore a slightly battered "NetWork Corp" logo across the front of it. He stroked his short, greying beard lightly as he reached back into the car grabbing a black travel mug with a picture of the classic 'Munster's' cast from the old TV show printed on the side of it. His sneakers crunched along the sidewalk as he set out towards the building as morning sunlight glinted and shifted across the sidewalk before him as it filtered in through the multihued yellow, red, and brown leaves of the surrounding trees. Already the grass began to yellow, and the leaves began to drop as the season upon which those things that were once deemed necessary had come to a close and nature preened itself of these unnecessary accessories.

The thinly carpeted entryway boasted a few chairs for people who were waiting for appointments to sit upon as well as a now dust-covered front desk bearing the large, engraved logo "NetWork Corp" along its front. Along the opposite wall sat a broken automated check-in kiosk, a haphazard and pathetic gesture provided by upper management during the crazy days of the pandemic for 'contactless entry.' It displayed the same error message that had been burned onto its screen for the past few years with no one caring to fix it.

Adam sighed as he looked at the dust-covered front desk where a squat little metal bowl stood on one corner. "Hey Sherril." He said, speaking to the ghost of the kindly old woman who once worked there. "Halloween is coming up. I don't suppose you'll be filling your candy bowl anytime soon, though." He quipped with a bittersweet sigh.

Adam sipped his coffee as he passed through half-lighted hallways and corridors leading to dark, empty offices on both sides. The years that had passed since "two weeks to flatten the curve" felt like a surreal blur both incredibly fast and incredibly long at the same time. He turned a corner and stepped into a large room segmented out into tan cubicles with window-clear tops above which pale yellow lights flickered. He walked by stations in various states of abandonment ranging from completely empty to those still bearing calendars set to March of 2020 alongside dead houseplants.

Just beyond a pile of ethernet cords which sat coiled up like a family of snakes occupying one cubicle sat a cubicle workstation unlike the rest. Desk lamps stolen from a conference room provided a beacon of light across a station three times the size of a normal station. Heavy metal posters and horror movie icon decorations sat tacked up all around the station. Adam sat down his coffee and flicked his computers on letting each fire up the three screens it managed in turn. He sat down in the executive chair stolen from a corner office and pressed his lunch bag into what had once been a wine cooler, back when they had a club bar for after-work parties. It now resided under his desk serving as a makeshift minifridge. He pondered if this is what it would be like to live in a zombie apocalypse as he watered one of the three plants that he had taken from around the office using a bit of water from one of the dozen or so jugs he still had remaining in his collection.

The intra-office chat box came up on Adam's screen with one, glaring message across it.

Clarity Gates: "*Come to my office first thing in the morning.*"

Adam blinked at the screen awkwardly and swallowed down a bit of fear. What did Clarity, the company founder and president, want to talk to him about?.

Adam's heart pounded in his chest, and he rehearsed through several possible outcomes from this meeting as he walked through the silent, echoing halls to her office. "I would say I have been a great asset to this company over the past seven years that I have been working here and dispute any claims that my work has been slacking off." He muttered under his breath as he approached the stairs. As he ascended the stairs, he looked up at the colorful banner which still hung overhead announcing their successful service vector processing product launch. The light flickering through the bank of windows behind it caught and glinted its way across every surface. He smiled as he muttered "Why thank you, Dr. Gates, I appreciate the promotion and substantial raise which goes with it" Even as the words left his lips, Adam shook his head snorting with disgust, "come on, man. You know that's not going to happen. It would have been Brandon on group chat announcing your promotion." He sighed and pursed his lips. His gaze trailed off to the left across a bank of overstuffed armchairs and couches arranged loosely in a 'hang out' spot over which hung a large poster of Dr. Clarity Gates. She wore a sharply pressed hunter green suit over a high-necked blouse. Her eyes had the far-off stare of a corporate visionary and cold intelligence behind her eyes befitting a computer genius. Beneath her folded arms read the motivational quote, "our sacrifice becomes our greatness."

Adam didn't feel any comfort from these corporate platitudes, nor did he feel any ease looking into her slim, angular face beneath her straight, brown hair. Walking by her image rendered massive on a matte poster print made him feel even more fear that he would soon be stepping into the office of a god.

The tasteful waiting area outside of Dr. Gates's office bore fewer scars of the pandemic than the rest of the building. Whatever janitorial staff remained seemed motivated to dust and clean here. Also, more importantly, Lisa Manstoeffler, Dr. Gate's young, blonde assistant sat in the assistant's desk just outside of office. Adam hesitantly stepped up to the desk where Lisa sat typing furiously away on a computer keyboard. She wore a short, stretchy floral-patterned dress and could easily be consider beautiful had she not been so openly antagonistic towards him in the past. She looked up at him with a resentful glare that Adam had seen many times before. It was the suspicious stare of disgust that all women, especially young and pretty ones, give men the first moment they meet. Adam groaned internally. Even with only three people left in the building, Lisa always managed to make it feel as if the space wasn't big enough for both her and for him. Worse still, she appeared to be in an even fouler mood today than usual. Adam chalked this up to an unfortunate twist of fate. The delicate curves of her cleavage and slight pout of her lips testified to her beauty while her clenched teeth and angry eyes bespoke the bitterness in her heart.

Adam steeled his nerve and pressed forward with the patently insane act of pantomiming the motions of an office building operating in the before times. He cleared his throat before saying "Hello, Lisa, I'm here to see-"

"Yes, I know. Clarity is expecting you." Lisa snippily replied.

She pressed some keys and the oak door behind her opened automatically.

Slowly he peered inside the exquisitely bright room. Floor to ceiling windows covered two walls of the corner office casting rectangular slabs of light interspersed against the support beams of the building. Automated shades whirred and buzzed softly as they aligned themselves with the motion of the sun to block the bulk of the headache-inducing brightness. He blinked in surprise at the polished marble floor. This contrasted so starkly against the typical, thin, contractor's carpet and linoleum which covered the floors of the rest of the building that he pondered for a moment if this room still occupied the same dimension as the rest of the building.

“Come in.” a stern, female voice commanded from the right side of the room. He cocked his head towards it and saw a large alabaster desk of perfectly polished black slate upon which sat a series of computer monitors flanking either side that seemed to hover in mid-air with no visible wires or other forms of communication or power visible. Behind and centered between these sat Clarity Gates herself. She looked at him impassively with tight-drawn lips which conveyed no emotion at all. Her pristinely tailored dark-grey business suit and no-nonsense bun gave her an air of impeccable professionality the likes of which made Adam feel a deep unease within his soul. Still, he had no choice but to step into the room.

“Hope your resume is up to date.” Lisa hissed out in a scathing whisper as the door closed behind him.

Clarity glared with occasional blinks of light illuminating either side of her face from the computer screens on either side of her as Adam slowly shuffled his way in. He dreaded leaving unwanted footprints on the marble flooring with each step and felt an overwhelming terror descend upon his soul. The sense of misplacement, of not belonging pervaded his every pore as the very air of the angelically powerful and pristinely kept room felt as if it stiffened against his presence.

“Sit.” She commanded gesturing slightly towards one of the two slender, steel chairs which sat incongruously in front of her desk.

As if in a twisted, floating nightmare, Adam slowly sat on one of the chairs looking at Clarity the entire time. She sat quietly for a moment letting the overburdening weight of silence fill the room like an elephant that no one speaks of. Adam dared not move, much less speak.

"Do you know why I called you in here?" Dr. Gates said with preponderant weight on her words. Adam's heart pounded in fear, but he wisely shook his head not daring admit to some unknown wrongdoing on his part. Dr. Gates said "Mr. Carpenter, when I started NetWork Corp everyone, and I mean everyone, told me it was destined to fail. Zuckerberg has his book of faces and Bezos his little South American river company, but there's a difference between those sad excuses for corporate technology billionaires and me. Do you know what that difference is?"

Adam swallowed hard and mumbled something.

"Speak up."

"I…uh… don't know, ma'am."

"Ma'am?"

"Uh, yeah, sorry. I don't know, Dr. Gates."

"Unlike them, I work for a living. I'm not just an overstuffed owner who sits on a yacht somewhere occasionally phoning in to work from time to time. I stay in touch. I stay in tune. While those cowards were hiding from the pandemic and arguing with employees over work from home privileges, I continued to be right here. Every day. Some days in an N95 mask, but I always showed up for work. There's a difference between an employee who has quiet quitted and is merely complying maliciously for their paycheck and one who is part of the team."

She swiped her fingers across the screen bringing up metrics collected on Adam. He saw the familiar listing of his prior, annual performance reviews as well as task completions and ticket closures.

"You… are a part of NetWork Corp's team. Not in some trashy Wal-Mart calling their employees 'associates' so they can justify slave wages, but really are a part of NetWork Corp's team. I'm aware of what you did for the Rio Tinto job."

Adam started to feel his heart rate decrease as she mentioned one of his more successful tickets. His voice returned to him as he cleared his throat saying, "yeah, that was a tough one. Those guys were pretty…uhh… intense."

"Mining uranium in the Democratic Republic of the Congo during a civil war is not a task that can be accomplished by people who are anything less than 'intense.'" Dr. Gates snapped back.

"Oh, uh… yeah… of course.' Adam replied.

"Add to all that the fact that you came back. As soon as the office re-opened, you returned. Why?"

Adam shrugged and said, "I figured that I was in just as much danger at home as here. I might as well get stuff done, for what I can do, I suppose."

"You do not have to cut yourself short to impress me." Dr. Gates replied sharply.

Adam clenched his teeth. For being 'complimented' in a seemingly 'good' meeting, he sure had a knack for messing this up.

"Uhh… yes… I understand, Dr. Gates." Adam replied sheepishly wisely opting to keep his mouth shut beyond this statement.

"We have a problem, though, Adam. You're an excellent employee who has proven yourself time-and-time again but…" Dr. Gates slid her lithe fingers across the screen bringing up metrics and analytics on all of Adam's internet activities both at work and at home. His face blanched as he saw a number of his favorite pornography sites flashing in red close to the top.

"I honestly don't understand why anyone would look at porn. Surely, you've seen a naked person before, why bother looking at naked people again."

"You were tracking all that?" Adam asked his throat shivering in fear.

"Yes, I've seen a great deal of your sexual… diversions." Clarity Gates said with a bitter snarl. A few more swipes and the screen transitioned to a capture of Adam as viewed through his laptop webcam and simultaneous capture of the screen before him.

Adam ducked his head in shame as Clarity Gates watched the ghost in the machine of Adam's masturbatory past pleasuring himself along to an intense femdom video.

Adam kept wondering if he was going to wake up soon and prayed to whatever god would listen that this whole thing was just a terrible nightmare.

Clarity let the clip play. He glanced up at her face trying to read any emotion in it as she sternly watched the video of him rolling his head back and an irregular squirt of cum flying upwards from below the view of the screen.

She turned the video off and once again let the weight of terrible silence fill the glistening and beautiful room.

"Shit." Adam whispered as he shivered in anger. Anger at himself for having been so callous and stupid with his internet usage. Anger at his own lack of self-control which led him to make such reckless and dumb decisions even while at work.

"Normally, you would be fired by now." Dr. Gates said.

"I'm… not?" Adam replied in confusion.

"I don't have the same emotional attachments towards sexuality that plagues the minds of weaker women." Dr. Gates said.

Adam looked up at her. It felt strange looking her in the face, a face he had only ever seen before magnified to god-like proportions but now one which stared back at him with all the full humanity of an existent person.

"I don't think you're disgusting." She said, quietly.

Adam held his silence. She continued, "It's normal, female cowardice to see a man succumbing to sexual weakness and to flee either physically or emotionally write him off as wretched. I'm not prone to such cowardice. Weakness does not build empires and cowardice blinds a person from the truth. What I see is an overall good employee who needs one thing corrected."

"It won't happen again."

"You and I both know that it will."

Adam swallowed hard.

"Perversions are nothing more than simple biochemistry. You know what I mean. Sexual desire is nothing more than testosterone, dopamine, serotonin and oxytocin. Chemistry, Mr. Carpenter, nothing more than chemistry." She brought the video up again and freeze framed it on the frame of him orgasming. Adam held a hand over to cover it saying, "Can we not look at that?"

"Why? You are merely looking at yourself and I've been looking at it all morning. I even showed it to my assistant, she's a bit weaker than me, but such is to be expected of an underling."

"You showed this to others?" Adam demanded angrily.

"This was filmed on my cameras by a person working in my corporation using my internet connection." Dr. Gates said back to him her voice wavering on the edge of anger.

Adam trembled as she took a moment to collect her composure.

"You have been, and still are, a good employee. You have so much potential. When I look at you, I see the same creativity and intellect necessary to be successful in this world and…"

She reached across the table laying a lithe hand on his own. Adam tensed at the unexpected physical contact and stared up into her eyes. He noticed a strange passion burning behind them as she continued "I want to cultivate that potential in you, Mr. Carpenter. I want someone by my side at the top of the company. Someone I can trust."

"By your side?" Adam asked in surprise. She smiled at him and said, "the title can be whatever we make it but, yes, I am hoping to have you by my side as second in command and an equity partner with substantial ownership in the company."

Adam gaped at her in awe and her smile turned sad as she let go of his hand saying, "this behavior, however, is a problem we need to fix." Dr. Gates said gesturing towards the screen.

"Fix?" Adam asked.in trepidation.

Dr. Gates said "Yes, fix. You have a pair of small organs which cause you to make bad decisions. We remove them and the bad decisions will stop."

"Whoa, whoa, you want to cut off my balls?" Adam gasped.

Dr. Gates scrunched up her nose and said "Cut? No, no, no, don't be ridiculous. What is this, the middle-ages? We will not do anything so barbaric as cutting off your testicles."

Adam blew out a sigh of relief as a small chuckle rose in his throat before Dr. Gates continued

"We'll burn them off with a laser."

Adam blinked "you're kidding, right?"

"I'm not kidding. We have a class four laser down in the chip manufacturing bay which can cauterize flesh in less than a second. Won't take any time at all."

"This can't be real" Adam protested.

"Our sacrifice becomes our greatness, Mr. Carpenter." She replied.

"No, this is insane. You can't force me to let you laser my balls off."

"That is true. In that case, you are fired and must leave the premise immediately. I will inform HR to keep this video recording of you sexually molesting yourself during work hours to provide to any interested parties requesting a professional reference on your behalf."

"Whoa, whoa…" Adam held up his hands defensively at her. She cocked her head to the side inquisitively.

"Give me time to think about it, okay?"

Dr. Gates pouted lightly and replied "I don't understand what there is to think about. I'm offering to remove your sexual frustrations and make you senior partner. Any other man would just at such an offer."

"Yeah, but, my balls."

"You can keep them, if you like. I suppose we could find a jar or something that you can put them in."

"No, what I mean is…"

Dr. Gates leaned in and said "Adam. Please don't make me second guess my intuition about you. I thought you were stronger than this. It's an obvious fix for a minor inconvenience."

"My balls are not a minor inconvenience to me" Adam protested.

"Of course, they are. It's not like you have a girlfriend or a wife. In fact, my touching your hand there just now was the most contact a woman has ever made with you for years."

"How, how do you know?"

She flipped through the monitor to bring up his reddit posts and complaints.

"Do you spy on all employees."

"Of course not! What, you think I have nothing better to do with my life? No, Adam, in fact I wouldn't have even noticed your diversions had it not been for the fact that I was actively looking at you to bring on as a senior partner."

"Why me?" Adam asked. He jerked his head out towards the empty office saying, "why not just promote one of the VP's or the CFO or something?"

"People do not climb the corporate ladder by being competent at their jobs. They climb the corporate ladder by being sharks in suits who stab people in the back. I'm not like them, I didn't climb to the top of NetWork Corp, I created it. I need someone competent that I can trust." She flipped through a few more screens saying "I reviewed everyone in NetWork Corp, everyone, from CIO to the janitors and you alone stood out above the rest, so I began digging a little deeper. It wasn't all bad. I like that you're a Leo, by the way, it matches well to my being a Capricorn."

Adam scowled lightly in confusion. To his surprise, a slight blush passed through Dr. Gates's cheeks before she continued "if you believe in astrology. Which I obviously don't."

"What I am proposing is jointly working on a multibillion-dollar, multi-national corporation. This isn't punching a timeclock for a paycheck. The kind of relationship I'm proposing is even more intimate and with even higher stakes than marriage."

She gestured towards his crotch saying "if you were getting married, you would be granting one-woman exclusive access to your sexual organs and one woman alone losing their ability to be used with other women. To become my partner, you have to sacrifice distractions."

Adam mulled the maddening thoughts in his mind.

"I will be with you, every step of the way. Especially afterwards. This sacrifice you're making on my behalf will not go unrewarded and, once your mind has cleared, I am excited to get to be intimately connected with you as we work on my-"

She stopped and a smile spread across her face which looked downright friendly as she continued leaning forward towards him as she said, "*our* creation together. A man and wife create meager babies. So, what, the world has billions of people, what's a few more. You and I will create the most powerful company on the planet. Money will be on endless tap. Governments will bow before our power. I've researched you deeply, Mr. Carpenter, and I've decided to give you the opportunity to be part of my life."

"this… this all feels unreal. Is this a prank?"

"Do I look like the kind of woman who plays pranks?" Dr. Gates replied sternly.

She pulled up a piece of paper typed up in trim legal language on company header. She lay it out in front of him saying "meaningless contracts drone on for pages while meaningful contracts say what they mean and nothing more. Read through the contract and see that it is to your liking."

Adam reviewed the surprisingly short legal document carefully. It laid out himself as receiving a controlling share of NetWork Corp as well as all the other details exactly as Clarity had promised him. "This doesn't say anything about my balls, though?" Adam said twisting his mouth hesitantly.

"I declined to pass the issue of your testicular removal through NetWork Corporations outside legal representatives for, what I hope, are rather obvious reasons. You may sign now, if you wish. I, however, will only countersign once I have your balls in my hand."

Adam shivered as he swallowed hard. On one hand, this simple sheet of paper would propel him to a life of power, wealth, and prestige beyond his imagination. He would indeed belong in a room like this. On the other hand, it would mean sacrificing his manhood. He stroked his short-trimmed beard thoughtfully as he considered the proposition. He knew that Clarity Gates's plan of making the video of him jerking off at work part of his professional reference was not an idle threat. No one rises to the top by being nice to everyone and Clarity was well known to have utterly destroyed a few people along her meteoric path to wealth. Even in the current employment environment, having the 'pervert' tag added to his description would utterly ruin any hope he may have for a future career.

But all of this had a cost. His manhood. Wouldn't it be better to be penniless and still have sex than wealthy beyond imagination and a eunuch? Adam thought back through his sexual past and pain dredged through his every thought.

Every cold and frustrating night.

Every 'high maintenance' girlfriend who bankrupted him financially and emotionally.

Every bad decision and bitter ex.

It all just…

wasn't

worth it.

This epiphany brought fresh resolve to Adam's mind, and he signed the contract quickly before doubt could change his mind and destroy his one and only chance at success.

"You made a good choice, Mr. Carpenter. Though…" Dr. Gates leaned towards him. For the first time since he had sat down, he noticed the faint outline of her cleavage barely visible in the dark recesses of her suit jacket. "…given our new relationship, may I call you 'Adam.'"

"Uhh… yes."

She smiled back warmly saying "Excellent." She leaned back with a happy, alleviated smile on her face which seemed strangely out of place. She blew out a sigh as if she had been holding her breath during the entire exchange and perhaps throughout the duration of her life as she said "finally, I'll have someone."

"Have someone?" Adam asked in confusion.

"You have no idea how long I've been looking for you, Adam. Oh well, we'll have plenty of time to discuss that later. For right now, let's get your manhood taken care of. I'll have Lisa take you down to the factory floor-"

"Wait, Lisa is going to take me?"

"Just to help you get setup and to give me some time to reprogram the laser. I'll be down in a bit. Don't worry, I will be the one to personally castrate you. I don't know why I'm feeling so excited about it. Maybe I'm just looking forward to being with you so much."

Adam gritted his teeth and said "maybe."

The office seemed to blur and warp around him as he stood. Suddenly the dreamy feel of the blinding white office felt strangely appropriate as did his deal with the devil at the black desk of moral superiority but now the time to pay his due had already come and it would be payment in advance. Even worse than that, Lisa would be part of it.

By the time he left the office, Lisa had apparently already received the memo. She stood up as he stepped into the foyer and a shocked look spread across her face. Gone was the hatred and resentment, now her mouth gaped in utter surprise and the moment the door closed behind him she hoarsely whispered, "You agreed?"

Adam blinked at her. Apparently, Clarity had shared a great deal of information with Lisa prior to the exchange with him.

"Yes." He said.

She shook her head and said "But… but… you couldn't have agreed. I mean… you'll never have sex again. You know that, right?"

"I know."

Lisa raised a hand to cover her chest as she seemed to pant in confusion unable to cope with the world shifting reality she now faced. Adam scowled. She seemed to have a great deal emotionally invested in his firing. Some part of the façade that lay between them seemed to crumble in that instant. They no longer looked at one another as the assistant to the top boss and an unknown drone from sector seven-G. In the gaping silence of dropped professionalism between them a strange sense of calm entered Adam's heart. He finally found courage to ask her the question he had always wanted to know.

"Lisa. Why do you hate me so much?"

Lisa swallowed hard and twisted her lips for a moment before admitting, "because Clarity likes you."

Lisa trembled as she continued "every fucking day, I keep hearing about how brave and dedicated you. She keeps talking about how you came back." She looked back up at him with her eyes beginning to water as she continued "I came back too. Does my bravery count for nothing?"

"You wanted this job?" Adam asked.

"Oh, God, listen to you talk. It's not a fucking job, Adam. It's a whole god damn life. A life that people like me can't even dream of."

"People like *us*, Lisa." Adam replied. He gestured towards the downstairs saying, "don't pretend that my job down in engineering is any more glamorous than yours."

Lisa looked off distantly and continued, "No matter how hard I worked. No matter how much she confided in me…"

Lisa gave a defeated gesture saying, "she liked you. Always you. Watching your perverted acts of self-molestation with her this morning made this the best day of my life. I assumed you were fired, but her insane demand felt like the next best thing. I knew, *knew* you would never sacrifice your precious manhood for any amount of money Clarity promised. But…"

A pained expression crossed Lisa's face as she gritted her teeth and asked, "how could you?"

Adam shrugged and replied, "you said it yourself, it's a life that people like you and I can only dream of."

Lisa took this in quietly.

She reached up and wiped a tear away from the lower edge of her eye.

Adam continued, "Look, you have a lot to unpack here so I'll just go find the factory floor sector myself."

"No. I will do my job." Lisa spoke with quiet resolve.

She blew out a sigh and continued "I suppose if Clarity had asked to cut my ovaries out for a promotion, I would have quit on the spot. Maybe you are as dedicated, or perhaps crazy, as she thinks you are."

Lisa stepped out from behind the desk saying, "besides. You'll be my boss soon. I should get used to following your orders." As she approached him their height difference became apparent as she looked up at him. She grimaced as she continued in realization, "oh, shit, you'll be my boss and I've been mean to you the entire time."

Reflexively, Adam reached out a hand and placed it on her shoulder to comfort her. The moment he did so, she looked at it and he instinctively pulled it back realizing his mistake.

She blinked at him inquisitively and he nervously clenched his hand a few times feeling regret over having touched her. He was already branded the office pervert. He surely didn't need to make it any worse.

"thanks, for telling me why you hated me. I feel better knowing that it wasn't something that I did. I…" Adam trailed off. No element of this conversation could be remotely construed as normal. He continued "I'm not angry at you for hating me. I suppose if I was competing against someone as hard as you were competing against me, I would hate them too.

She smiled sadly and replied "You won. I lost. I suppose there's no point in being a sore loser."

Adam cocked his head lightly and replied, "says the woman who gets to keep her genitalia."

Lisa nodded and she reached over onto her desk and grabbed up a banded hair-tie. It bore a metal pink and white petaled flower decal attached to a black elastic band. Adam tried not to stare as her breasts naturally bulged upward with the motion of her smooth arms as she collected up her hair and tied it back in a simple yet elegant ponytail. "I suppose that is too bad, but you must admit that *is* your fault."

Adam frowned as Lisa gestured for him to follow her with a tip of her head towards the elevator. He felt the warmth of her sensual body beside his own as they strolled through the dead office. Her floral perfume, now free to waft about with the motion of her body, filled his nostrils with its intoxicating scent. His wandering eyes couldn't help but glance little snippets of her Lisa spoke up saying "It's strange to think what would drive you to do something so stupid though, when you seem a powerful adversary-" she stopped and corrected herself saying "…a reasonably intelligent man. I mean, do you really crave women that badly?"

Adam shook his head as they approached the elevator. She pressed the call button as he replied, "I… don't know. It's hard to explain."

The elevator arrived and they stepped inside, quietly perching on opposite walls facing one another in the cramped box as it descended. Lisa quietly folded her hands behind her back and rested against them along the elevator wall. Her pale, smooth upper chest and arms seemed to glow against the dark beige wall behind her. The smooth, tight floral print skirt portion of her dress hugged against her curvaceous hips terminating demurely just above her knees. Adam desperately tried not to notice the singular point of sensual life in the abandoned office building this as they rode down the elevator together. Lisa disallowed this.

"Have you ever craved me?"

Adam blushed and asked "huh?"

Lisa leaned forward letting him see her smooth rounded breasts poking out from the dress more fully as she continued, "I'm just curious, I mean, you're madly perverted and have insatiable cravings for women. I'm a woman so I just want to know if you ever had your perverted thoughts about me."

Adam trembled lightly.

Lisa leaned back a bit and gave him an impatient stare. She continued, "Adam, our boss is about to shoot your balls off with a laser. This isn't a 'should I report you to HR' type question. I just honestly want to know."

Adam eventually found his voice replying with a cringe "a little"

Lisa's face brightened with a smile. He couldn't tell if it was a 'gotcha' smile of triumph at forcing his admission or some other kind of smile, so he quickly back peddled saying, "but you always hated me so much that I just… well… pushed you out of mind for the most part." Lisa's smile fell a bit and she said, "I suppose that is too bad, I must admit that is *my* fault." She shrugged and said "We both have our vices, Adam. You have your perverted desires and I have my burning anger. Yours is going to be fixed by surgery." She pursed her lips thoughtfully before she muttered the rhetorical question, "what can be done to fix mine?"

Her tone turned serious as she continued in a determined voice, "I vow, as your soon to be employee, to do better at handling my anger." She stood up a little straighter coming away from the wall saying "starting right now. I've been so wrapped up in myself and losing out on this promotion that I haven't really been thinking about how you must be feeling. You are literally losing your entire sexuality today…"

She trailed off for a moment before picking up again saying "Adam, while you still have your genitals, is there anything you would like to do with them?"

Adam swallowed hard and went wide eyed unsure how to answer such a question. Lisa stepped in a little closer to him with a pleasant smile on her face saying, "I would be happy to help."

"Help?" Adam asked feeling his head swim with emotions.

With an oddly misplaced positive attitude, Lisa continued brightly saying, "Of course. I'm a woman. I have my birth control and your files didn't indicate any venereal diseases. You've had perverted cravings about me. It would be better for both of us to start off our new working relationship on a good footing, rather than you resenting me for never getting a chance to live out your fantasies. So, what kind of perverted cravings have you had? I'll help you live them out until Clarity gets done programming the laser to cut off your manhood."

Adam raised a hand and it hovered trepidatiously over Lisa's shoulder for a moment. She smiled at him reassuringly and said "go ahead. You can touch me. My only rule is you're not allowed to hurt me…"

She then coyly pursed her lips, and a fresh blush came over her face as she stared off dreamily for a moment before continuing "…that much."

She bit her lower lip and her whole body seemed to shiver in strange anticipation as she continued in a breathy whisper "I suppose you can hurt me a little… if you like."

Adam grabbed hold of her warm shoulders and pulled her soft, warm body in close to his own. He knelt his head and said to her "kiss me."

Lisa obeyed leaning her head back and letting Adam drink from the lips that which, up to that point in time, had only ever been used to say hurtful things at him. After a few seconds of the kiss, she began to giggle slightly which caused Adam to release the kiss.

"What?" he asked.

"I never kissed a man with a beard before. It's soft and tickly just…" Lisa shook her head and bit her lip muttering "makes me wonder what it would feel like elsewhere. But that's… no… no… this is for you."

The elevator came to a halt and the door slid open with a ding. Adam released his grip on her, but Lisa let her hand slide down to clasp into his own as they stepped out. "I'm a bit surprised you started with a kiss. I figured you were just going to force me to my knees and make me start sucking your cock." Adam shrugged and responded, "what can I say? I'm a romantic at heart."

He nodded to her hand saying, "so we're holding hands now like boyfriend and girlfriend or something."

Lisa surveyed the basement with a squint as she continued, "It seems reasonable to hold your hand. I'm waiting for you to take me to the place where you're going to abuse my body for your sick, sexual pleasures." Adam swallowed hard not knowing how to take the twisted simultaneous invitation and insult. He likewise began looking around the basement.

The good news was he now had a girl willing to fuck.

The bad news was the setting was less than ideal.

Blank white doors under flickering fluorescent lights peered out at them behind which sat an array of full-body clean-room suits in a cramped dressing room for employees to use before entering the chip-making factory floor. Doors to the right led to a small, dingy single bathroom and another door to the left led to a modest office with a large bay window looking out over the factory floor. Long before the ravages of corona virus this facility had already fallen victim to the forces of economy and cheap chip production in India. As such, it had lain dormant years beyond the rest of the building and had been purposefully mothballed rather than hastily abandoned. Exploring the area for ghosts came to Adam's mind, but the warm feeling of Lisa's hand in his own stabilized his mind upon the purpose.

"Office" he said gesturing towards the door on the left.

"Oh, thank god, I was afraid you were going to fuck me in the bathroom." Lisa replied quickly and then clenched her teeth as if she had said something wrong. They walked hand in hand over to the office door. She held up a finger as she looked at Adam continuing, "Don't get me wrong. I would be willing to have sex with you in the bathroom."

"Bathrooms are cramped and smelly." Adam muttered as he pushed open the office door ignoring the now defunct finger-print scanner and keypad alongside it.

"Exactly" Lisa replied.

Fluorescent lights buzzed to life as they entered the office. Swivel office chairs sat at empty desks. A few remnants of technical papers sat tacked up on the wall at intervals and random odds and ends of office equipment lay strewn about haphazardly on the various desks. A large, ominous window sat off to one side beyond which only darkness could be seen from the empty factory floor. Most usefully, a prominent, wooden conference table sat in the middle of the room.

"it's perfect." They both whispered in unison.

Lisa turned towards Adam and smiled sweetly saying "You have the girl. You have the room. What would you like to do with me? What is something you've always wanted to do, but were afraid to ask openly?"

Adam stepped in close to her and lovingly caressed his hand under one of her ample breasts feeling the softness and the heft of it. She looked down and smiled at his hand. Submissively, she made no move to stop him as he continued to massage her for a moment before reaching around with his other hand behind her and grasping the zipper of her dress along her back. He gently pulled and she offered no resistance as her dress slid slowly open across her back revealing her bra strap as it went. He then reached up and took hold of one of her dress straps and slid it off her. She quietly tucked her arm in letting the floral cloth slink over her shoulders. Under his pervasive touch, the clothing which had defined her status as a working professional not to be trifled with soon crumpled to the floor leaving her standing there in her underwear. Her pale skin contrasted sharply against her black panties while her cotton white bra held her breasts up in a deliciously fleshy puddle.

Lisa muttered sheepishly, "I didn't know I would be having sex today. Otherwise, I would have matched my underwear colors."

"It's fine." Adam replied as he beheld all of her smooth skin which had been previously forbidden from his eyes. Her cute little belly button, her lush, firm hips, her sweet body. "You already know that I'm more interested in what's underneath the underwear than the underwear itself, right?" Lisa nodded and a furtive look of trepidation crossed her face.

"Are you scared?"

"No."

"Are you?" She asked back.

"Yes."

She smiled at this. "I suppose I would be too. I'll help get my body ready for you." She reached up and unsnapped her bra from behind letting it slide off over her shoulders and letting her gorgeous breasts flow out freely. Adam caught her breasts in his hands and ran his thumbs over her sweet, pink areolas for a moment before playfully caressing her nipples. He knelt down and brought one of the delightful morsels into his mouth where he suckled on it feeling the smooth nipple flex and warp on top of his tongue as Lisa moaned lightly in pleasure. He felt her shift and looked down to see her sliding her panties off for him and stepping awkwardly out from her clothing which now lay as a piled heap on the ground. She wore nothing more than her navy-blue strapped heels. Adam felt content to let her keep these on as they served to heighten her sexuality rather than detract from it in any way.

As he continued to suckle the forbidden breasts his fingers slithered down across her delicate skin in search of an even greater, secret prize. Her moans became more insistent as he slid his hand across her abdomen feeling her cute belly button pass beneath it. She lay her arms gently across his shoulders to steady herself as he continued his exploration of her body. He rotated his wrist downward and felt the small tuft of neatly trimmed pubic hair before a pair of warm, fleshy lips presented themselves to his fingers. She began panting in anticipation as he enveloped her womanhood between his fingers for a moment. He released his suckle of her breasts and looked her full in the face. Her eyes had softened from their hateful glare all the way down to doe-soft and dreamy. Her cheeks blazed red, and her mouth hung slightly slacked open.

"Are you really prepared to let me in here?" he asked.

"Yes." She whispered.

He pressed a finger in feeling the soft lips spread obediently open presenting a beautiful wetness the likes of which he had seldom experienced before. Her eyes fell shut and her head lulled backwards weakly as a quivering gasp emanated from her mouth for a moment.

"It's been a while since you've had sex, hasn't it?" He asked her.

She weakly nodded. "I almost forgot what that first touch feels like."

"And I've forgotten what touching a woman feels like." Adam

replied with a sad smile.

He curled his finger deep inside her pussy and she gasped. "Come along." He said. He stepped away but kept his finger plunged inside her. Lisa's heart pounded hard in her chest as the pervert tugged her body deliciously along pulling her quite literally by her womanhood. She kept trying to tell herself that she was just fulfilling his sick desires as a strategic business maneuver. Why then was her pussy getting wet? Why did her insides quiver? Were his twisted desires rubbing off on her?

No surprise crossed Lisa's mind as he directed her to lay on the table. The very act of sliding her naked body up onto the table seemed surreal and staring up at the bland drop ceiling as she felt the cold wood press against her buttocks and shoulders filled her with a sense of disappointment. Adam grabbed up her ankles and lifted her feet up onto the table after her folding her knees upwards while her strappy shoes clicked against the table just beneath her womanhood. Lisa felt no urge to take her shoes off either, if anything they helped her feel a bit sexy and powerful even with the depraved acts she must now endure for the sake of her career. Lisa let her legs fall open invitingly as she expected her womanhood to be penetrated shortly. She closed her eyes preferring darkness to fluorescents and waited to hear his pants unzip.

Something tickled her left knee. She looked down and saw the top of Adam's blonde hair as he knelt and kissed the inside of her knee. She pursed her lips wondering what was going on until the second kiss came, this time further up along her inner thigh. All the while, he kept his hands wrapped around her feet creating a strange dichotomy between the warmth of his fingers pressed between the hard leather straps of her shoes. Lisa's body caught on to where he was going before she did as the third kiss, this time nearly halfway up her inner thigh sent shivers of anticipation through her frame forcing her to close her eyes. She focused her energy on the nearly insurmountable task of turning off her rational mind.

Don't overthink it. Just let the pervert have your body and enjoy the rewards. Lisa internally reminded herself.

Adam helped as a fourth kiss landed near her crotch and she felt the faint, wispy hairs from his beard and locks begin tickling across her womanhood and abdomen. This unlocked her body's desire, and she groaned letting go of all the cold, analytical, rational thoughts. Her breath ran rapid and hoarse as she quivered awaiting the location of the next kiss and the sweet, sensual feeling of his tongue caressing her womanhood. She felt him shift and a kiss…

…on her right knee.

Internally her cucked body screamed in agony at its denial. Her womanhood was right fucking there, why did he skip to her right knee? Now her rational mind had to quell the vapid beast of her own body in reminding it that he was merely building up anticipation and would be licking her shortly. She felt the kisses come same as before, bit by bit up along her inner thigh. Her heart pounded loud in her chest as he made his final kiss just along the inseam of her crotch. She felt his hair dangling down tickle and caress across her abdomen as he shifted and kissed…

Her belly button.

"Damn it." Lisa grunted out under her breath.

"Did you say something?" Adam asked.

"No, just… I… well…"

"What?"

"This is supposed to be about your perverted desires, and so far, everything you've done is just so… well…"

"Just so… what?"

"Normal."

"You're just pissed that I haven't licked your pussy yet."

"That's not it at all."

"If you must know, I'm exploring your body. Getting to know it. Think of me like a tourist looking at the national monument from every angle."

She arched her head to look down at him as he let go of her feet with his right hand and began running it along her body touching each part as he spoke saying "smooth, silky legs, soft, tender belly, warm voluptuous breasts." His voice dropped as he leaned down whispering "sweet, wet, pussy." Lisa moaned as he finally pressed his tongue into her pussy licking deliciously at her clitoris. Her back arched and delicious warmth spread through her abdomen. After a few provisional licks, however, he stood back up and looked at her firmly. She panted lightly and looked back at him as he continued "For you these are just boring things you see in a mirror each day. For me, though, they're beautiful and exciting so, yes, I'm exploring a bit."

Lisa bit her lower lip and replied, "you don't have much time, though, Clarity codes fast." She felt his thumb press into her pussy as he replied "I suppose you're right. You sure you don't have any perverted desires?"

"Of course, I don't." Lisa replied quickly with a blush.

Adam slowly released her feet and put them back down. He reached out a hand and pulled her up to her feet. Lisa blinked in surprise. Was that all? Had she done something wrong?

"We're a bit limited on supplies here so you'll need to help me live out my perverted desires with you. Go pick out two paper binder clips from the office supplies."

"Binder clips?" Lisa asked in confusion.

"For your nipples."

Her eyes went wide as her hands went up to her mouth in shock. Adam continued calmly "you've been mean to me for a long time so, yes, I do desire to hurt you at least a little." Lisa swallowed hard and dropped her hands down in defeat. She had, after all, agreed to this.

Adam leaned in and continued, "Now we both get to find out how brave you really are. Are you going to be a coward and come back with a few little paper clips or are you going be a real woman and return with the large clamping kind. I'm going to get undressed while you search so off you go."

Conflict filled Lisa's mind as she walked awkwardly naked through the empty office as Adam stripped off his clothes behind her. A part of her wanted to watch him strip while another part of her wanted to grab her dress and run away. She resented being forced to go retrieve her own instruments of torture and yet, at the same time, her body seemed to buzz with fresh electricity at the prospect of what was about to be done to her. Some deep and primordial urge felt strangely awakened by the thought of participating in her own pain.

Her rational mind railed and yet she quelled it reminding herself that no matter what little bit of pain he put her through it would be nothing compared to what he would soon experience under Clarity's laser.

True to his word, the challenge presented itself as she beheld a wide array of sizes of binding clips all scattered together on a desk. Logic dictated grabbing the smallest ones she could find but Adam's challenge to her womanly bravery rang within her ears. To Lisa's surprise, she found herself picking carefully through several of them testing the level of clamp they had by squeezing the curved metal wires spread out behind a few times. She pouted thoughtfully like a woman trying to select the best shoe. Some of the largest ones felt like they had so much pressure they might shear her poor nipples clean off, the smallest were clearly a good way to get branded a coward and so that left her with the midrange. She tested several of these glancing over her shoulder briefly to see if Adam was distracted enough for her to try them on herself before he clamped her. It felt oddly a great deal like shoes, she wanted to try them on in the store before letting a man see her wearing them, but this was more a way to gauge her own degree of stoicism and pain tolerance. Playing with the clips in her fingers was one thing but the dread image of him putting the clips on her and her squealing like a pathetic little girl ran through her mind and the urge to test them first filled her body.

"Find any?" the call came out.

"Umm… yes." Lisa replied over her shoulder.

It was too late.

She had to tempt fate and face how strong she really was in front of the man who would soon be her boss.

She grabbed some of the larger mid-range clamps deciding it better to fail at pain tolerance than to not even succeed at trying and obediently returned to Adam.

It wasn't that she truly desired to stare at his cock the moment she turned around but rather more that she simply could not. It twitched erect in firm excitement and the knowledge that this odd feature of men would be having its way with her soon enough made Lisa shudder even more than the steel clips in her hands. Otherwise, his body appeared pretty much the way she had expected it too. If anything, she was even more taken in by his hair, long blonde locks that maintained a volume that even she would like to have. She made a mental note to ask him what conditioner he used sometime later when he wasn't sexually abusing her body. As she drew near, she noticed that he had very much so undressed, even going so far as to fully unlace his shoes.

"Good girl." She heard him say as she presented the clips. A strange lightness entered her heart at the words. He tested the clips and raised an eyebrow at her saying "you are brave, aren't you?"

"I didn't want to skimp on your fantasies." Lisa forced her mouth to reply while her mind silently prayed to any god that would listen to not let her collapse to the floor and piss all over herself once the stiff steel jaws of the clips clamped down on her sensitive nipples.

"Turn around." He said firmly.

Lisa twisted her lips not sure why he was having her turn around, but she followed his instructions all the same. She felt him grab her hands and lay one wrist over the other. As she felt the fabric of his broad lace shoestring slide against her skin her heart skipped a beat, and she gasped looking over her shoulder at him. She wanted to protest but she reminded herself that this was still what she was giving over to him. Silence filled the air as he looped the laces around her wrists several times making as broad a band as he could with what little length of cord that he had available before cinching them down tight leaving her hands bound behind her back. She gave a provisional wriggle and found her hands bound fast with no hope for moving them. He then grabbed her shoulders and turned her back around smiling at her.

"Gorgeous." He said to her.

Lisa repressed a smile. She didn't want him to know that somehow having her hands tied behind her back leaving her vulnerable to him did, in fact, make her feel sexy. She stood there passively as he warmly caressed her left breast puddling it up in his hands. Soothing sensual pleasure emanated from the warmth of his touch on her sensitive skin. She almost wished he wasn't doing this because she knew what was to come next. The odd irony of the fact that she was having sex with him only just before he was to lose his balls floated briefly through her mind, but the idea came caught short as he brought up the first steel clamp. She watched quiet and tense as he massaged her nipple with his thumb, probably the last good feeling her nipple would experience for the time being. He pressed open the clip and brought it up to her. She felt her delicate skin slide unwittingly into the steel jaws of the clamp and held her breath in terrified anticipation for a moment before he released his grip on the tension letting the clamp close in on her nipple. Icy waves of pain emanated immediately from her poor nipple and seemed to spread across first her entire breast and then pierce bitterly through the rest of her body. Lisa's body spasmed and she nearly doubled over as she hissed through clenched teeth trying to resist the urge to cuss loudly or beg him to take the clamp off. She felt grateful that he had tied her hands, first because had he not she would have instantly grabbed the clip off her own breast, and he would have probably made fun of her for it.

"Deep breaths." He said sounding eerily helpful and encouraging with the torture he was putting her through. Lisa did just that, breathing the pain down to a manageable level and getting herself back to standing upright again. She reminded herself that this was his last chance to experience sexual pleasure, no matter how pervasive, and that the pain she was experiencing was helping her gain forgiveness from the man who would soon have great power over her life. She straightened her shoulders and arched her back pressing her breasts forward bravely. Fear slithered through her mind as he took up her other breast in his hand and began warmly massaging it. The fact that what she had just experienced would soon happen again rattled in her brain and she didn't know if she could bear the stress of such horrific pain from both breasts. She didn't get the choice as she felt the steel jaws take her last remaining delicious little nipple into their embrace and squeeze anguish through her body once more. This time, she fell to her knees with a whispered "motherfucker" on her lips.

Unable to hold herself up, she rested against his legs terrifyingly aware of how close to his cock her head was. She felt his hand come down and rub her back reassuringly. She looked up at him glancing at his cock briefly and she saw him smiling back down at her. "Brave girl." He said to her.

She leaned her head against his thigh breathing deeply trying to cope with the excruciating pain spreading outward from her nipples. She swallowed hard and whispered, "Do you hate me?"

"No." he replied.

"You offered your body to me for my desires. It's too bad you'll never get a chance to see yourself like that, bound up and in pain. It's the sexiest you will ever look in your life."

His tone changed as he asked, “are you going to wimp out?”

“No. I promised I would fulfill your perverted desires and I will.” Lisa said firmly.

Something about that position, that bondage, that pain began to work weird wonders on Lisa’s body. Yes, her nipples hurt sorely but already they were growing accustomed to their newfound pressure. The closeness of his cock, with its smooth purple tip and intricate pattern of veins felt more like a promise than a threat.

He gently cupped the back of her head and directed her around to in front of him. She knew what was to come next as he whispered to her “Open wide.”

A strange comfort came over her mind, body, and soul as his warm, fleshy cock entered her mouth. It felt somehow strangely connecting, or perhaps grounding to her. Maybe it just gave her a welcome distraction from the agonizing pain in her poor breasts. Still, exploring the smoothness of his tip with tongue brought a warm murmur of appreciation to her lips and a fresh dampness between her legs. For his part, he oddly busied himself with the remaining shoestring looping it down below to the wire handles on the clips holding her nipples squeezed tight in agony. Every movement brought fresh little titillations of pain forcing Lisa to focus all her attention on not biting down on the cock which she feasted upon sensually. In short order, Adam righted himself and a gentle tug came at her breasts. Lisa’s eyes darted about as she could not see all of what had happened, but he held a curve of the string in his left hand and with every motion a fresh tug from the clamps on her nipples pulled taught indicating that he had indeed tied the string to her nipple clamps and was now using it to direct where she should go.

Adam looked down at the beautiful blonde assistant, a woman way outside his league, now on her knees wearing high-heels and nipple clamps that he held her by. The ministrations of her mouth felt delicious beyond words as she sweetly suckled his cock. He reached down and caressed her cheek saying, "look up here." She did, giving him a submissive stare as she continued suckling. He smiled back at her reassuringly. "you're doing great. Sucking the cock of the man who has you in pain." He cupped his right hand behind her head just below her flower-banded ponytail and pulled taught on the strings pulling her in to a deeper suck as his cock pressed further and further into her warm, soft, mouth. "Yes, that's good. A little deeper is perfect. You're going to keep sucking nice, sweet, and deep until I fill your beautiful little mouth with my cum. Then you'll drink down all my salty cum as your own private little snack."

Something about his words filled Lisa with a surreal conviction. Her pussy throbbed and her nipples ached as she lapped her tongue urgently against his frenulum ushering out the prize which would soon be hers. He began to moan and thrust back and forth inside her mouth in a sweetly pulsing rhythm that made her regret that it was merely her mouth that he was thrusting inside of. A loud moan left his lips as he leaned back against the table for support came right before the salty flavor of success filled her mouth. A younger her would have been afraid but she had come too far and suffered too much to give up now, so she suckled more lightly drinking down his cum as she went. It felt as if she was swimming in him, indeed nearly drowning in him and soon she had to break the hold of her mouth on his cock and gasp in greedy breaths of oxygen as she collapsed unable to hold herself up any longer without the aid of her hands.

Adam released his grip on the string about her nipple clamps and let her fold down at his feet as he pressed his hands on either side of the table for support. The trickling streamer of cum still lazily drizzled from his cock as his knees felt like jelly. "You can rest. You did…"

he panted before continuing "…very good." He swallowed hard and tried to compose himself. His heart pounded so loud in his chest he feared it would fly out at any moment. A faint whimpering seemed to be coming from Lisa as she murmured wordlessly from the floor. Adam knelt and gently took hold of her shoulders helping her back upright. Lisa's mouth quivered lightly as thin tears formed in either corner of her eyes. "You were amazing."

Lisa swallowed hard and pursed her lips as she seemed to tremble all over her body. It almost looked as if some crack had formed in her previously impenetrable armor, and she now lay nearly exposed for the first time in her life. A strange mixture of curiosity and pity crossed Adam's mind as he beheld this sight. He decided he must be seeing things wrong. Intuition was never his strong suit to say the least. "Let's get those clamps off you. No matter how sexy you look wearing them, perhaps you were a bit too brave, and I did promise not to hurt you too much."

He slid his hands under her shoulders leveraging her by her armpits to help lift her feeling her soft, warm breasts press gently against his arms. He leaned her up against the table and she flopped backwards across it letting her legs slide submissively open as she went. Adam marveled at how she now offered not even the faintest hint of resistance to him and all they had done so far was some light BDSM and a simple blowjob. Carefully, he pinched the binder clips open carefully removing them from the already red and sore looking nipples they held in their clasp. As he did this, Lisa groaned wordlessly unable to speak the strange sensations which were passing through her body. He gorgeous, smooth breasts and deliciously tortured nipples were too much for Adam to resist as he took turns suckling at each one before blowing it dry to cool the sore and sensitive flesh. Lisa gently writhed and whimpered as he did this pressing her hips out further in expectation. Finally, Adam ran a hand down along her smooth little belly and to her pussy once more. It felt different from what it had before, and he blinked in surprise as she nearly squealed the moment his finger grazed her clitoris.

"Do you have a girl hard-on?" He asked.

Lisa trembled.

He stroked again and she gasped with a fresh tear beginning to form anew in her moist eyes. Her eyes, however, were not even a fraction as damp and languid as her pussy which seemed to be dripping with excitement.

"Looks like I'm not the only one with perverted desires." He whispered with a chuckle.

"I'm just doing my job." Lisa lied as much to herself as to Adam. She looked down at him and said, "I'm just letting you live out your fantasies with my body while you still have the balls to do so."

"And this?" Adam said as he ran his fingers gently up through between her labial lips leaving an explosion of sensitive pleasures in their wake and nearly pressing all intellectual thought. She took a moment to collect herself before replying.

"Natural… biological response…" Lisa gritted her teeth for a moment before continuing "It's just my body responding to being used for pleasure. It doesn't mean anything about me."

"And if I said I had my fun, and we were finished?" Adam teased. Lisa's eyes went wide, and he chuckled "don't worry." He slid his body in between her sprawled legs and took hold of either side of her hips. He lined her up and slid his cock deep inside her womanhood. It almost looked like her neck was spring loaded as, at the exact same time he plunged sweetly into her womanhood, her head tilted back, and a gasp of exultation mixed with relief left her lips.

"Better?" He asked.

"if it's what you want." Lisa replied trembling at the cognitive dissonance of her own words.

"Hey." Adam said intimately.

Lisa looked down at where he stood between her legs cock skewered deep inside her body but not yet thrusting. A strange moment passed between them. One of strange intimacy as he took hold of her hips saying "you're allowed to enjoy this, okay. I sure as hell won't tell Clarity anything and I won't think any less of you for having a good time."

"Really?" Lisa asked.

"Absolutely."

Adam pressed slowly deeper inside her feeling every delicious inch of her womanhood swallow up his cock hungrily. He replied "You're probably getting sore from being tied up still. I'll get that rope off your wrists."

"No. leave it." Lisa replied quickly.

"Huh?"

A blush came over her cheeks as she continued, "the rope, well, makes this easier. This way I don't have to worry about what I'm doing with my hands."

Adam smiled and said, "that's one way to look at it. It also makes your breasts stick out nice and perky. Very beautiful." He reached up and gave one a gentle squeezing massage. He continued "I've cum in women and made women cum, but I've never experienced a woman cumming on me before. Just feeling her writhe, tremble, and orgasm while on my cock. Something on a bucket list, I suppose, but now is my last chance." He put his hand to his mouth and licked his thumb saying "Since your clit is so nicely swollen, that's what I'm going to do with you next. I'm going to stroke your girly erection until you cum all over my cock."

Lisa's eyes went wide as she silently watched his thumb descend to between her legs.

"Gag me."

"What?"

"I don't want to say anything stupid. Just… please…"

Adam blinked in surprise but looked down at the ground. He held up a finger saying, "I'll be right back." Lisa's body protested angrily as he withdrew his cock from her driving her to jolt and shift with a gasp at the sudden cold, hollow feeling in her abdomen. He returned with her stretchy floral dress rolled up into a long coil. He quickly slid it beneath her head serving as a strangely impromptu pillow for her momentarily before joining both ends into a knot tied over her mouth. Lisa's heart relaxed as the warm confines of fabric encased her preventing her from speaking.

"Better?"

"mmHmm" Lisa murmured in agreement before feeling the delicious, warm, filling sensation of his cock press deep inside her body once more. She happily rested her head back staring briefly at the glaring fluorescents overhead as she felt his wet thumb touch lusciously against her starved clitoris breathing sweet life into it with even the subtlest of strokes. Gratitude for the gag filled her heart as even just a few strokes later upon her delicate nub of nerves left her nearly howling with pleasure into the gag about her mouth. True to his word, he did not thrust as this would be an act that would pleasure him rather he simply held his cock inside her body reassuring her hungry pussy that it wasn't alone as he played eagerly with her clit conducting a symphony of pleasure that only she could hear in the veins and sinews of her core and one that he experienced the pulse of as her hips flexed and jostled all of their own accord yearning to be taken. Lisa found herself wishing he would thrust, take her body as his own, squirt his cum deep inside her pussy. Girly parts of her began fantasizing about getting pregnant, having his baby, being his wife, becoming his for ever and ever. These parts prattled on while the rational parts of her mind knew none of this was going to happen nor was it what she really wanted to happen. She entertained the fantasy, however. Same as the paradise of the warm body penetrating her felt infinitely better than the hard table she lay on or the glaring lights blazing down from overhead, this girlish fantasy felt sweetly satisfying.

Lisa lifted her legs and wrapped them around him as best she could. She placed her feet on his buttocks and flexing her thigh muscles to draw him deeper into her core. She panted and moaned into the knotted wad of her dress crammed in her mouth and pleaded him to fuck her right to motherhood, give her a baby, and marry her for all time being. The glory of safety encompassed her as the stretchy fabric did not care about the barely intelligible words that she was speaking into it and Adam could hardly make out any actual words at all from her lips between the moans and screams. She let the fantasy play out as he played a game of sexual pleasure using her body which sweetly succumbed to his desires leaving her bucking and screaming manically out of control of herself unable to process much less cope with the overbearing sensory overload of pleasure. Wetness began to trickle along her thighs and Lisa realized it was not his wetness, but her own as her womanhood had just squirted on his cock covering it with her own bodily juices. The cavalcade of pleasure began to subside lightly as he took his turn and began thrusting deep inside her already over stimulated body. She had nearly collapsed in exhaustion when she felt his cock grow powerfully thick inside her body and begin squirting thick, delicious cum deep within her womanhood. This brought fresh quivers of pleasure to her as she felt her body succumbing to his use of it for his pleasure.

Adam shuddered and collapsed into a nearby spinning chair as Lisa still lay there on the table with her legs dangling helpless over the edge occasionally quivering in the aftershocks of incredible pleasure. He looked across her soft, smooth body, now wet and trembling with pleasure and he wondered how long his luck would hold out. So far, he had experienced much of the joy that Lisa's body had to offer and no sign of Clarity yet. He took a deep breath to strengthen himself as he rose up on wobbly, sex-drunk legs. He nearly collapsed on the table next to her as he reached across it towards her head and unknotted the dress from her mouth releasing her voice once more. She gasped at the air as trembling shocks flowed through her frame and her eyes quivered along half-lidded.

"What… next?" Lisa managed to pant out.

Adam's eyebrows went up in surprise.

Then a smile spread across his lips. "you're still up for fulfilling my fantasies?"

Lisa swallowed hard and nodded.

"come off the table." Lisa shimmied lightly as Adam pulled her along sliding her off the wooden table. She fell onto wobbly legs, and he took a seat in the office chair gesturing towards her saying "lay across my lap, face down."

"Are you going to… spank me?"

"yes."

A wry smile spread for the briefest of seconds across Lisa's face before she forced it away and dutifully spread her soft and wanton body over his lap feeling his cock, slightly relaxed after their sexual adventures so far, pressing lightly against her thigh. She stared disinterested at the industrial grade carpeting beneath the chair. It felt odd to be laying across another person's lap with her ass vulnerably up in the air especially as a grown adult, but some perverse and childish part of Lisa actually enjoyed it. Just like the clips, it felt like a challenge and even the consummate professional within her felt a bit of satisfaction at the act of a job well done. Adam stared down at the gorgeous woman's buttocks laying across his lap just beneath her tied hands still clasped together behind her back. Lisa wiggled her bottom slightly causing it to jiggle in the most arousing of manners. Adam couldn't tell if this was her trying to balance herself or trying to entice him. Either way, it was working.

"Since this company punishes perverts, it seems you need punished too. You, and your gorgeous, rounded ass needs to be punished."

"Yes, sir." Lisa replied in breathless anticipation.

Smack

The sound seemed to explode through the stillness of the dead office room followed by a short yelp of pain from Lisa's lips which she bit back before it could manifest as anything more. Adam smiled in awe at not just the feel of her sensually soft ass cheek against his hand but at how it bounced and jiggled when he hit it.

Smack

This time she whimpered as he slapped her other butt cheek reaching across her tight little crack. She whimpered and Adam felt something wet spread submissively across his right thigh from where her vulnerable pussy leaked slightly of both her and his own juices. He twisted his lips up as this gave him an idea.

Schallop

This time Lisa arched her back and moaned in pleasure. Adam didn't remove his hand after slapping her this time as he had smacked her right between her legs slapping across her taint and letting his fingers smack her labial lips. He kept his hand there and slid a finger into her pussy feeling its wetness and comfort as her body shivered at the memory of pleasure. Bravely, he pressed his thumb into her ass making her tense up in fear.

"you have one last hole to give me. Will you?"
Silence.

"Yes." Lisa said breathlessly.

Adam looped his arm under her chest tipping her back up onto her feet. She looked at him with doe eyes as he smiled at her and turned her around facing away from him saying "have a seat in my lap."

It took a few tries to line her up properly but soon Lisa found herself being pulled down onto his lap feeling a stretching pressure welling up in her buttocks. Something about this act, this final submission, felt incredibly cathartic. Her tired legs shook as he guided her ass down inch by swollen inch along his cock which felt like a powerful rod driving itself into her body as he went. She dared not let her legs give out, however, and collapse onto him suddenly because she didn't think she could take him all in at once in such a quick time. Pain came and she gasped as her ass protested the growing cock within it. Adam supported her weight with his arms for a bit as she breathed through it and then they continued. After what felt like an eternity, her buttocks came to rest on top of his thighs as his cock pierced deliciously inside her frame. Adam grabbed either side of her beautifully wide thighs feeling the incredible tightness of her ass and began thrusting inside her in slow, continuous pulses. Lisa shivered and whimpered leaning her head back across his left shoulder as her body rose up and down slightly on his lap under the constant pulse of his thrusting. She groaned as his thrusting grew faster in tempo as his cock plumbed deep inside the recesses of her body where it wasn't normally supposed to go but to where she had allowed it to go anyhow. A strange feeling of intimacy crossed Adam's mind as her soft hair lay splayed across his shoulder and her head rested on him while he continued thrusting inside her wonderfully tight ass. Like some strange and primordial part of her being knew that she could trust him to take what he wanted from her body without truly harming her. Intense pleasure built up within his cock as her ass grew slick and inviting inside losing its resistance to his penetration. He reached around and grabbed across her breasts with one hand so he could experience one last touch of her beautiful womanhood before his final cumming. A scream, some blend of pleasure and pain, emanated from her mouth as he frantically began thrusting inside her. She made no move to escape as her body, a powerful machination of pleasure which she had not truly unraveled its full potential prior to that day, took in Adam's cock and brought forth once more a torrent of cum as he exploded into pleasure deep within her ass.

She gasped and whimpered as he slowed down his tempo while his cock flexed and squirted deep inside her body. Sweat trickled down her forehead as tears formed across her eyes and her body shook intensely. Adam drew a deep breath as he slid her slickly off his cock and let her collapse on her knees in front of him.

He reached down and untied the shoelace from around her wrists returning free use of her hand again as she watered the carpet with her tears.

"I never…" she whimpered.

"Did I hurt you too much?" Adam asked in concern.

She shook her head and raised herself up using her hands to look at him from hands and knees on the floor. She blinked and said, "I never knew I could do that." She wiped away some tears and continued "Even with my boyfriend, I had never done such things. And now with you, I…" She shook her head and said "All the things I could have experienced for the first time with someone I loved but was afraid to, and now I did them with you. And…" She swallowed hard and shook her head trying to chase away her next sentence.

"And you're angry about that?"

"No. I'm not angry. I'm just dissapoin-"

She cut herself off quickly and furrowed her brow in frustration for a moment.

She continued in a formal tone, "I hope that I served you well."

Adam smiled. "You were amazing. My only regret is that it won't ever happen again."

Lisa smiled lightly at this and said "yeah."

"Are you going to be, okay?" Adam asked seeing how she seemed so distraught over their exploits. Lisa chuckled lightly and replied "Yeah. It has definitely been an interesting day at work, to say the least."

She reached down and caressed her hands across her body saying, "next time you look at me, you won't feel anything at all." She pouted lightly and continued "I'm not sure how I feel about that, to tell the truth. I hope you remember what we did today, though."

"How could I forget?"

A voice pierced the blanket of derelict silence surrounding them from the end of the room shouting out "What the hell are you two doing?!"

Lisa screamed in terror and quickly covered herself with her hands desperately trying to protect what little was left of her demureness.

Clarity glared at the two of them with a look of shocked horror on her face for a moment before recomposing herself.

"I'm so sorry. I was just…" Lisa blubbered fearfully as she backed away towards her dress.

Clarity rolled her eyes, "unable to keep your panties on, I see."

"No, no, it's nothing like that." Lisa whimpered.

"I asked her too." Adam spoke up.

Clarity glared at him. He continued "I practically begged her to have sex with me just so I could experience it one last time."

"What?" Lisa whispered to him in surprise.

"You're right. I need to get my balls taken off. That way I don't abuse your staff anymore."

"*Our* staff." Clarity spoke in a reminding tone.

Clarity gestured towards Lisa saying, "be that as it may, Lisa, I would be hard pressed to find the activities you were engaged in down here listed on your official job duties."

"No, they wouldn't be." Lisa replied sullenly with her head downcast.

Clarity continued "I would expect this behavior from a man, but I thought you had more sensibility and professionalism than to waste time with such behaviors."

"Please, don't be hard on her. I made her do it." Adam pressed.

Clarity glared at him, and her eyes flickered down as she frowned bitterly continuing "and those balls poisoning your blood with testosterone made you do it. The sooner we get them off you, the better. Come on then. You might as well leave your clothing here. You need to be naked for this anyhow."

Clarity snorted at Lisa saying "put your clothes on and get back to being a professional woman rather than a woman of the world's oldest profession. Clock out the last thirty minutes. These shenanigans down here were your morning break. You were off the meter for them. I'm sure as hell not paying you to sleep with men."

"Understood, Dr. Gates." Lisa whimpered as she quickly began gathering up her clothing. Clarity exited and keyed in her code at the factory floor. Adam bent over and picked up Lisa's bra off the ground and handed it back to her. She seemed curled up in a ball of bitter embarrassment and humiliation.

"I'm sorry." Adam whispered to her.

He then pursed his lips for a moment before resting a supportive hand on her shoulder. She looked up at him and he continued "once I'm partner, I'll do what I can to get you better treatment. I'll make sure you don't get in any further trouble for today." Lisa sniffed back a tear and asked "really?"

"Sure, after you shared your body with me today so generously and fulfilled all my desires. Of course, I'll look out for you." Lisa smiled sadly as she slid her bra back on saying "I suppose I can trust what you're saying. Especially since you already tried to take the blame for me just now."

She looked off distantly as she reached behind her back latching her bra back into place. She continued as she looked intimately into Adam's face saying, "I would have just let you get fired." A somber look crossed her eyes as she continued, "I would have enjoyed it too. Laughing bitterly at your loss."

"Oh, dear God. Clarity did make the right decision in offering the position to you instead of me. Didn't she?"

Lisa sighed as she began hiking up her panties over her legs again. Once she had slid them safely into place, Adam replied, "you didn't have to give me a final experience of my life today, but you did. You recognized what I needed and took care of it. Thank you for that."

He pulled her in to a warm and intimate hug which she returned wrapping her small arms around his large frame. Down beneath, his cock began to rouse lightly in the presence of Lisa's pussy despite the panties separating them. Her pussy began to salivate again slightly, but they both ignored their sensual desires for the time being. This wasn't a hug of sexual pleasure. It was a hug of intimate understanding. For Lisa's part, it felt good to be hugged and held. Those girlish desires to marry and make him her own danced about in her heart but for the moment she felt edified by the simple power of his acceptance of her. An acceptance she could not extend to herself. For Adam's part, gratitude filled his mind at the wonderful things she let him experience with her body. Also, a strange sense of odd kinship with his former enemy welled within his heart.

"Good luck." She whispered in his ear as she lightly patted his back.

"Thanks." He replied with a sad smile.

"lay down there." Clarity commanded starkly as Adam approached where she worked furiously away at a screen attached to a massive assembly line. The semiconductor factory floor lay in intermittent patches of light and dark from the partially operational beams overhead. A series of steel and rubber industrial lines, each flanked by complex machinery and large warning signs, spread across the floor. Given its mothballed status, they both flagrantly ignored the line environmental requirements forgoing both the dust-free 'bunny suits' as well as the mandatory static-electricity bands which would attach to the ankle and slide under the worker's shoes to electrically ground them at all times. As Clarity worked, an overhead mechanism whirred to life and descended towards the assembly line. Adam shivered lightly as he looked at the device which would end his manhood. He had imagined something akin to a ray gun but instantly chastised his stupidity as he beheld the metallic box mounted on robotic gears and plastered with warning signs which swung into place over the line. Naturally, this made more sense than his imagination conjured up. Under manufacturing conditions, great care was taken to ensure no worker accidentally stuck their hand, or in this unimaginable case, their balls, under the class four laser cutting tool. Clarity pressed a few more buttons and the box lifted away from the assembly line making space for Adam to lie upon it.

Clarity looked at him firmly and said “well, come on. Get on the conveyor belt.”

Adam frowned and asked, “is this safe?”

“Of course not. What part of ‘I’m removing your testicles’ was unclear? It is purposefully unsafe. We are not utilizing this machinery in an OSHA approved application today.”

“Yeah, I know, but will it…uhh… burn or cut anything else?”

Clarity seemed to brighten at this saying “We could put your penis in there too, if you like. I suppose from an aesthetic point of view it would be better to simply have a completely smooth crotch.”

“No. I would…” Adam cringed and swallowed hard continuing “I would like to keep my penis.”

Clarity shrugged and replied, “Fine by me. It won’t work without your testicles anyhow.”

Gingerly and with great trepidation, Adam climbed up onto the assembly line. His shoulders and hips extended beyond the line onto the framework on either side of the static Teflon belt. He stared up at the black ceiling above punctuated in about three areas, from his point of view, by sharply angular directional overhead lights. He felt strangely blinded by the contrasting dark and light above him such that he turned to look at Clarity. She stepped over to him and he saw she had a series of ratchet tie-downs on hand. She began to loop a set over his naked chest.

"What are you doing?" Adam asked in protest starting to sit up.

She pressed him back down and said "I can't have you moving around while the laser is cutting your balls. Just stay still and trust that I know what I'm doing."

"Do you really?"

"Of course, I do. I'm a genius who raised this company from the ground up. I can do anything." Clarity replied haughtily.

Her crisp business suit seemed oddly out of place both against the manufacturing floor as well as contrasted against Adam's own full nudity. He looked at her carefully trying to get a read on the situation. Her face held firm in detached concentration, but her lithe, small hands told a different story. He looked down at them as they slowly slid across his chest caressing the broad, orange nylon strap over his body. The humiliation of being tied down by a woman so powerful blended with the fear and oddly soothing caress to create quite the impact on Adam's body and mind.

"Why is it up?" Clarity asked in a demanding tone.

Adam looked down across his own naked body strapped to the conveyor belt and at his own erection "It just is."

"Well make it go down."

"I can't. It's just… kind of does its own thing."

Clarity stared at his cock then back at him. "It just looks so wrong."

"Somethings wrong with me?"

"No. Just… a penis and testicles in general. Having reproductive organs flopping around outside of a person's body. Parts of it even you can't control. It's hard to believe that this chaotic mess of sexuality is the best evolution could come up with."

Clarity reached down and wrapped her fingers around his cock unintentionally spreading pleasure with her touch. She seemed to stand their contemplative for a moment before she whispered, "it feels so… warm." She stared at his manhood in fascination. Instinctively, her thumb brushed across his smooth head and his cock twitched in response. "it's alive." Clarity gasped and released her grasp of his cock before shivering lightly in embarrassment at her own ridiculous act of naivete.

"Have you never seen a man's cock before?" Adam asked slowly.

"Of course, I have." She replied with a snort before frowning and continuing softly "they…uh… had… anatomy books in college." She began stepping back towards the controls.

"You've… never had sex before?" Adam asked feeling odd incredulity overcome him as he asked the question.

"I was building the future. Boys are a liability with absolutely no return on a woman's investment."

Adam lay there quietly unsure of how to respond to that. Clarity looked off distantly for a while before pursing her lips and lowering her eyes. Some part of the armor she seemed to always wear about her started to crack open a bit. She stepped away from the controls and back over to Adam. The box hung ominously overhead but Clarity leaned against the factory line right where his hips lay. She looked at Adam's erect cock and then back up to his face.

"While other girls were learning to wear makeup, I was learning how to write code." She sighed and looked up across the darkened factory as she continued "I went straight from books to business and lived in my first office building twenty-four hours a day seven days a week."

"Visionary, passionate, driven, domineering…that's what men call me." Clarity frowned and continued sadly "Sex is simply something that has never been part of my life."

"I'm… uh… sorry to hear that. I guess?"

"Yes, which is why I am concerned that you failed to answer my first question." She nodded towards his cock saying, "My weak-minded secretary is no longer here for your amusement, so why is your cock erect?" She turned towards him. Curiosity filled her voice as she scowled inquisitively at him asking "Is it because of me?"

Adam tensed up as he looked at her. Her face softened a bit as she lay a hand on his shoulder saying "Your answer isn't going to change your fate. Just be honest. I don't want our relationship to be marred by secrets. Just tell me why your penis is erect."

"I… don't know. I should be scared. I know I should be scared because you're going to burn my balls off with a laser, but I can't help other than to feel… well… a bit turned on by you being the one to end my manhood." Clarity cocked her head to the side. She looked off for a moment before muttering "that doesn't make any sense." She blew out a sigh before continuing "but part of business acumen is adapting to conditions on the ground. You're aroused by your own castration. I just have to accept that what you say is true." She smiled and continued, "I suppose it is something for you to look forward to. You'll never have to worry about sexual frustrations again." She gingerly reached down and tapped her forefinger against the smooth head of his cock. It reflexively flexed at her touched straining to encounter the sensation again.

"Huh? Did you move it?"

"No. It just does that on its own."

She gave a weak smile saying "for what it's worth, once I get over how abominable male anatomy looks in general, I suppose it is rather handsome, for a penis that is. It's probably a good thing that Lisa got to enjoy it. She has been under a great deal of stress lately. It's too bad I just can't…"

"Can't… what?" Adam asked.

Clarity shook her head and said "Nothing."

"I don't want our relationship to be marred by secrets." Adam said.

"Huh?"

"You're asking me to give up my balls, at least you can finish your sentence."

She stared at the controls for a bit before glancing over at his cock. She stood there for a long while in deep thought before sighing in exasperation and blurting out "Fine. I'll find out what all the fuss is about."

Adam watched in amazement as she reached up under her skirt and removed a pair of black cotton panties sliding them down over her legs and taking them off along with her shoes which she unstrapped and left next to one another on the floor along with her panties folded up neatly on top of them.

Adam's eyes lay plastered wide in amazement. Although she still wore the same business suit and skirt as before, he knew she wore nothing underneath. She looked down across her own body before looking over at his.

"A boyfriend would distract me. A husband would demand a prenup and take half my hard-earned shares. Any prostitute I hire would blackmail me."

She sidled up next to his body and gingerly reached out grasping his cock with her left hand. He felt her warm, small fingers wrapping around his manhood. "If I left you intact, it would change the nature of our relationship. Sex can't be part of the equation for my plans to come to fruition but…" Clarity gently massaged his cock feeling it twitch and swell between her fingers. "One time, just this once, I'm going to satisfy my curiosity with the only man I can do that with. Don't get any big ideas, though. I am not going to succumb to your perverted desires like my weak-willed secretary."
She slowly climbed up onto the assembly line while Adam watched quietly. She swung a knee over and straddled his legs for a moment. Something about the fold of dark cloth of her skirt spreading between her legs and the promising warmth beneath it roused him even more so. She looked up at him asking "What does it feel like to have a man's cock inside you?"

"I wouldn't know. Most women say it feels like being filled or fulfilled perhaps."

Clarity nodded asking "are you okay with me taking you inside."

"Yes."

Clarity smiled as she slid her hips up slowly centering her body over him. She began to sit, and Adam watched as his cock disappeared between the secretive black folds of her skirt. Her warm legs holding on to either side of him felt promising as her face leaned so close to his own, they could almost kiss. Sudden pain pressed against his smooth head as his cock accidentally jammed up against her inner thigh. He cringed but she reached down with her hand saying "Oh, I need to center you up right..."

He felt her soft, labial lips envelope the tip of his cock and she looked up at him with wide eyes of anticipation.

"Here." She whispered breathily.

She leaned up still holding his cock only very slightly within her body. "Point of no return." She whispered. She placed her hand on her heart saying "I've never been afraid of anything but why is my heart pounding? Why does it feel like strange electricity is going through my skin?"

She shook her head and said "You can do this, Clarity. Just…"

Adam moaned as her womanhood enveloped him inch by delicious inch within the sacred and mysterious confines of her dark skirt. The fact that she managed to have sex with him and still look exactly like she did on all the inspirational pictures amazed him a bit. For her part, Clarity gasped and then her mouth fell open as she whimpered.

"It's so…big… and…"

She came to rest sitting upon him with his cock planted fully inside her warm, tight body.
"filling. Yes, that would be a good word for it. Like I didn't know I felt empty until now I feel full." She began to rise and fall rhythmically spreading pleasure through both their bodies. "Imagine

doing this with someone you love. That would be incredible. I suppose I can see why all those girls and women like doing this now."

She wiggled slightly saying "what does that feel like for you?"

"Amazing." Adam croaked out.

Clarity smiled saying "Okay, big guy. How about this? I'm going to take your nuts off, but it doesn't mean it has to be a scary or miserable experience. You were turned on by the idea of me castrating you. I'll keep your cock safe and warm inside my pussy while I work on your balls. Just think of it, you get to have sex while being castrated. That's something you would enjoy, right?"

Adam nodded mutely.

"Good boy. I'm going to turn around so I can see what I'm doing." Sudden coldness rushed in as soon as Clarity pushed herself up from sitting on his cock. He gasped as she doubled over saying, "Oh, God. Ugg…" She took a deep breath and swallowed hard.

"Are you okay?"

"Yeah, I just pulled you out too fast." She shivered lightly and then began crawling about again in a circle around him. He saw the beautiful curves of her buttocks pressing outward against her dark skirt as she lined herself up again this time straddling him facing downward across his feet. She sat up and turned her head looking over her shoulder at him. A wry smile spread across her face as she asked, "Are you staring at my ass?"

"Umm."

"You are. Wow. Here…"

She hiked up her skirt letting the beautiful pale flesh of her shapely legs and buttocks come into sight. She spoke saying "go ahead and watch. The last you'll ever see of your intact manhood is watching it disappear into my body."

She sat down again, and Adam watched as her beautiful ass came to rest upon his stomach while her warm, wet vagina swallowed in his manhood deliciously. She groaned and said "that feels totally different. Like being filled in a whole new way." He could only see her back encased in her dark business suit, but he felt small fingers touching his testicles as she looked down at his balls which she scooped up in her hands. "All your problems by these two little organs." She began to rock her hips back and forth and Adam whimpered as he felt his cock moving inside her body. A strange pressure squeezed light pain against his balls, but it didn't feel like the heat of a laser, rather more almost akin to a crushing force but not quite enough to be truly painful. It felt like she hungrily bucked her womanhood against his balls saying "Oh, they feel so good rubbing against my clit."

She took a deep breath, and he felt her hand fall away from his balls as she continued "but I have to stop before I get addicted too and become just like any other woman." She reached up and brought down the laser box suspended as it was on the swinging robotic arm. She slid it up in between his legs saying "this is the best angle to work on you from, however. Your balls are neatly right in front of me."

He felt small fingers picking at his balls stretching his nutsack out lightly. He watched her cock her head to one side then the other as she delicately arranged his manhood so that it lay out in the best manner as to be destroyed. He cried out lightly as cold, metallic clamps fell into place around the base of his balls.

"Don't worry. Your balls are exactly where they need to be." Clarity said to him in a comforting tone of voice. She looked over her shoulder at him and continued as she began thrusting again "just focus on your cock. That will help with the pain. Just think about your cock nicely tucked up deep inside my womanhood."

Adam did just that, ignoring his clamped balls for the time being and enjoying the sensation of sweat, wet pussy swallowing and massaging his cock. Part of him wanted to reach out and put his hands on Clarity's beautiful, rounded buttocks but the ties around his wrists wouldn't let him. Rather he had no choice other than to let her take him where she was leading and right now, she was leading him towards either a castration or an orgasm. She moaned lightly saying "your cock is getting bigger inside of me. It must be because you're ready to get castrated. I suppose this is a bit exciting. One more button push, and your balls are burned off permanently in less than three seconds. Does that excite you?"

"Yes." Adam whispered breathlessly.

Clarity continued pumping up and down riding his cock and he felt like he couldn't hold his orgasm back anymore as she took up the controls saying "I'm going to give you a countdown to the end of your balls. Ready?"

"Three" Clarity called out.

Adam's cock stiffened and his balls lurched hard against their metal restraints.

"Two"

Adam's body trembled uncontrollably.

"One."

Orgasmic pleasure flooded through Adam's body as his cock began squirting hot, sticky cum deep inside of Clarity's womanhood. In the next moment she pressed the button and sweet, agonizing pain seared through his balls.

"Breathe through pain, Adam. Just breath through the pain." She said over her back at him as Adam lost all articulate voice at the simultaneous sensations and screamed in both ecstasy and agony at the same time. Three seconds felt like three hours as the razor-hot laser pulsed its way across his scrotum from left to right but like all good things it came to pass and soon Clarity pulled away the laser box and reached down onto the conveyor belt holding up a small, smoking piece of Adam's former flesh.

"You did it. You did it, Adam. Incredible!"

He felt her body slide off his quivering and shrinking cock as she rose up from her fucking position and slid off the side of the conveyor belt standing once more alongside him again. She held his nutsack, which smelled disturbingly like cooked ham, in her left hand. The laser had both cut and cauterized his flesh in one move leaving a perfectly sealed little pouch between her fingers with his former testicles inside. Tears trickled lightly down the sides of Adam's eyes as she marveled at his balls in her hand.

She looked up at him saying "Good job, Adam. I knew you had it in you." She gestured towards his body saying "the hard parts done. You did it. I hope having sex with me during the castration helped. I just…" She stopped talking and reached down between her legs with a sudden look of concern in her face. Her fingers came up sticky and wet. She pressed her thumb to her forefinger curiously a few times before asking Adam "Did you… cum inside me?"

Adam swallowed hard and managed to croak out a weak "yes."

Clarity's eyes went wide in terror as her body shook. "Oh god, oh god, Oh…."

"You… don't have birth control?"

"I never have sex, why the hell would I need birth control?" Clarity protested back.
She placed a hand on Adam's chest to hold her balance as she pitched forward slightly still holding onto his balls. She panted in fear for a moment before starting to recompose herself. "I did something to your body. You did something to mine." She looked off distantly saying "maybe it would be a little girl." Her face brightened lightly as she continued "I could teach her how to write code." Clarity nodded for a moment before continuing "as a final act of fairness, whatever is happening now inside my body, I'm going to let it happen." She looked at him intimately saying "if you managed to impregnate me with your final act as a man, it would be an honor to bear the child. I can handle the pain of it." She caressed the balls in her hand lightly saying "you handled pain for me. It's only fair. Agree?"

"Yes."

"Do you want to be an active father? That, is, if I'm pregnant."

"Yeah. That would be nice, but there's a good chance you aren't pregnant."

Clarity nodded saying "I know. I know. A lot of randomness in the process. A… uh… journey I never imagined I would go on."

She looked down across Adam's own smoldering crotch as she

continued "same as I sealed your fate for a journey you never imagined you would go on."

"What will happen to my balls?" Adam asked.

Clarity regarded them for a moment before replying "do you want them back?"

"Not… really." Adam said with a cringe of pain.

"Then I'll give your nuts here a nice new home inside a jar in my desk. A keepsake of our agreement."

"That sounds fair." Adam replied before leaning his head back and breathing deep the air around him.

"One question. What do you feel when I do this?" Clarity asked before lifting her skirt and showing Adam her pussy. He looked at her shapely legs and snug little womanhood. His mind conjured up all sorts of sexual fantasies however his body did not respond in the least to this.
"I don't feel anything."

Clarity dropped her skirt and giggled with glee saying "It worked. Wonderful." She hugged him from the side. He smelled her perfumed hair and felt her warm body press against his own, but these acts conjured nothing within his frame.

She reached over to a manilla folder she had left on top of one of the factory machines and pulled out the contract adding her own signature above Adams as she said, "You truly are the best partner any woman could ever have."

The faint gleam of a far-off nightlight gently illuminated Samantha's soft face as she lay curled up peacefully on top of her heating pad under a massive, fluffy, pile of blankets.

…and pressed 'send.'

Made in the USA
Columbia, SC
28 December 2023